I0550090

The Trembling of the Veil by W. B. Yeats

William Butler Yeats (1865 – 1939) is best described as Ireland's national poet in addition to being one of the major twentieth-century literary figures of the English tongue. To many literary critics, Yeats represents the 'Romantic poet of modernism,' which is quite revealing about his extraordinary style that combines between the outward emphasis on the expression of emotions and the extensive use of symbolism, imagery and allusions. Yeats also wrote prose and drama and established himself as the spokesman of the Irish cause. His fame was greatly boosted mainly after he received the Nobel Prize in Literature in 1923. His life was marked by his many love stories, by his great interest in oriental mysticism and occultism as well as by political engagement since he served as an Irish senator for two terms. Today, although William Butler Yeats's contribution to literary modernism and to Irish nationalism remains incontestable.

Here we publish his personal work of his journey through the years.

INDEX OF CONTENTS

PREFACE

I have found in an old diary a quotation from Stephane Mallarmé, saying that his epoch was troubled by the trembling of the veil of the Temple. As those words were still true, during the years of my life described in this book, I have chosen The Trembling of the Veil for its title.

Except in one or two trivial details, where I have the warrant of old friendship, I have not, without permission, quoted conversation or described occurrence from the private life of named or recognisable persons. I have not felt my freedom abated, for most of the friends of my youth are dead and over the dead I have an historian's rights. They were artists and writers and certain among them men of genius, and the life of a man of genius, because of his greater sincerity, is often an experiment that needs analysis and record. At least my generation so valued personality that it thought so. I have said all the good I know and all the evil: I have kept nothing back necessary to understanding.

W. B. YEATS.

May, 1922. Thoor Ballylee.

I

At the end of the eighties my father and mother, my brother and sisters and myself, all newly arrived from Dublin, were settled in Bedford Park in a red-brick house with several wood mantlepieces copied from marble mantlepieces by the brothers Adam, a balcony, and a little garden shadowed by a great horse-chestnut tree. Years before we had lived there, when the crooked, ostentatiously picturesque streets, with great trees casting great shadows, had been anew enthusiasm: the Pre-Raphaelite movement at last affecting life. But now exaggerated criticism had taken the place of enthusiasm; the tiled roofs, the first in modern London, were said to leak, which they did not, & the drains to be bad, though that was no longer true; and I imagine that houses were cheap. I remember feeling disappointed because the co-operative stores, with their little seventeenth century panes, were so like any common shop; and because the public house, called 'The Tabard' after Chaucer's Inn, was so plainly a common public house; and because the great sign of a trumpeter designed by Rooke, the Pre- Raphaelite artist, had been freshened by some inferior hand. The big red-brick church had never pleased me, and I was accustomed, when I saw the wooden balustrade that ran along the slanting edge of the roof, where nobody ever walked or could walk, to remember the opinion of some architect friend of my father's, that it had been put there to keep the birds from falling off. Still, however, it had some village characters and helped us to feel not wholly lost in the metropolis. I no longer went to church as a regular habit, but go I sometimes did, for one Sunday morning I saw these words painted on a board in the porch: 'The congregation are requested to kneel during prayers; the kneelers are afterwards to be hung upon pegs provided for the purpose.' In front of every seat hung a little cushion, and these cushions were called 'kneelers.' Presently the joke ran through the community, where there were many artists, who considered religion at best an unimportant accessory to good architecture and who disliked that particular church.

II

I could not understand where the charm had gone that I had felt, when as a school-boy of twelve or thirteen, I had played among the unfinished houses, once leaving the marks of my two hands, blacked by a fall among some paint, upon a white balustrade. Sometimes I thought it was because these were real houses, while my play had been among toy-houses some day to be inhabited by imaginary people full of the happiness that one can see in picture books. I was in all things Pre-Raphaelite. When I was fifteen or sixteen, my father had told me about Rossetti and Blake and given me their poetry to read; & once in Liverpool on my way to Sligo, "I had seen 'Dante's Dream' in the gallery there, a picture painted when Rossetti had lost his dramatic power, and to-day not very pleasing to me, and its colour, its people, its romantic architecture had blotted all other pictures away." It was a perpetual bewilderment that my father, who had begun life as a Pre-Raphaelite painter, now painted portraits of the first comer, children selling newspapers, or a consumptive girl with a basket offish upon her head, and that when, moved perhaps by memory of his youth, he chose some theme from poetic tradition, he would soon weary and leave it unfinished. I had seen the change coming bit by bit and its defence elaborated by young men fresh from the Paris art-schools. 'We must paint what is in front of us,' or 'A man must be of his own time,' they would say, and if I spoke of Blake or Rossetti they would point out his bad drawing and tell me to admire Carolus Duran and Bastien-Lepage. Then, too, they were very ignorant men; they read nothing, for nothing mattered but 'Knowing how to paint,' being in reaction against a generation that seemed to have wasted its time upon so many things. I thought myself alone in hating these young men, now indeed getting towards middle life, their contempt for the past, their monopoly of the future, but in a few months I was to discover others of my own age, who thought as I did, for it is not true that youth looks before it with the mechanical gaze of a well-drilled soldier. Its quarrel is not with the past, but with the present, where its elders are so obviously powerful, and no cause seems lost if it seem to threaten that power. Does cultivated youth ever really love the future, where the eye can discover no persecuted Royalty hidden among oak leaves, though from it certainly does come so much proletarian rhetoric? I was unlike others of my generation in one thing only. I am very religious, and deprived by Huxley and Tyndall, whom I detested, of the simple-minded religion of my childhood, I had made a new religion, almost an infallible church, out of poetic tradition: a fardel of stories, and of personages, and of emotions, a bundle of images and of masks passed on from generation to generation by poets & painters with some help from philosophers and theologians. I wished for a world where I could discover this tradition perpetually, and not in pictures and in poems only, but in tiles round the chimney-piece and in the hangings that kept out the draught. I had even created a dogma: 'Because those imaginary people are created out of the deepest instinct of man, to be his measure and his norm, whatever I can imagine those mouths speaking may be the nearest I can go to truth.' When I listened they seemed always to speak of one thing only: they, their loves, every incident of their lives, were steeped in the supernatural. Could even Titian's 'Ariosto' that I loved beyond other portraits, have its grave look, as if waiting for some perfect final event, if the painters, before Titian, had not learned portraiture, while painting into the corner of compositions, full of saints and Madonnas, their kneeling patrons? At seventeen years old I was already an old-fashioned brass cannon full of shot, and nothing kept me from going off but a doubt as to my capacity to shoot straight.

III

I was not an industrious student and knew only what I had found by accident, and I had found "nothing I cared for after Titian and Titian I knew chiefly from a copy of 'the supper of Emmaus' in Dublin, till Blake and the Pre-Raphaelites;" and among my father's friends were no Pre-Raphaelites. Some indeed had come to Bedford Park in the enthusiasm of the first building, and others to be near those that had. There was Todhunter, a well-off man who had bought my father's pictures while my father was still Pre- Raphaelite. Once a Dublin doctor he was a poet and a writer of poetical plays: a tall, sallow, lank, melancholy man, a good scholar and a good intellect; and with him my father carried on a warm exasperated friendship, fed I think by old memories and wasted by quarrels over matters of opinion. Of all the survivors he was the most dejected, and the least estranged, and I remember encouraging him, with a sense of worship shared, to buy a very expensive carpet designed by Morris. He displayed it without strong liking and would have agreed had there been any to find fault. If he had liked anything strongly he might have been a famous man, for a few years later he was to write, under some casual patriotic impulse, certain excellent verses now in all Irish anthologies; but with him every book was a new planting and not a new bud on an old bough. He had I think no peace in himself. But my father's chief friend was York Powell, a famous Oxford Professor of history, a broad-built, broad-headed, brown-bearded man, clothed in heavy blue cloth and looking, but for his glasses and the dim sight of a student, like some captain in the merchant service. One often passed with pleasure from Todhunter's company to that of one who was almost ostentatiously at peace. He cared nothing for philosophy, nothing for economics, nothing for the policy of nations, for history, as he saw it, was a memory of men who were amusing or exciting to think about. He impressed all who met him & seemed to some a man of genius, but he had not enough ambition to shape his thought, or conviction to give rhythm to his style, and remained always a poor writer. I was too full of unfinished speculations and premature convictions to value rightly his conversation, in-formed by a vast erudition, which would give itself to every casual association of speech and company precisely because he had neither cause nor design. My father, however, found Powell's concrete narrative manner a necessary completion of his own; and when I asked him, in a letter many years later, where he got his philosophy, replied 'From York Powell' and thereon added, no doubt remembering that Powell was without ideas, 'By looking at him.' Then there was a good listener, a painter in whose hall hung a big picture, painted in his student days, of Ulysses sailing home from the Phaeacian court, an orange and a skin of wine at his side, blue mountains towering behind; but who lived by drawing domestic scenes and lovers' meetings for a weekly magazine that had an immense circulation among the imperfectly educated. To escape the boredom of work, which he never turned to but under pressure of necessity, and usually late at night with the publisher's messenger in the hall, he had half filled his studio with mechanical toys of his own invention, and perpetually increased their number. A model railway train at intervals puffed its way along the walls, passing several railway stations and signal boxes; and on the floor lay a camp with attacking and defending soldiers and a fortification that blew up when the attackers fired a pea through a certain window; while a large model of a Thames barge hung from the ceiling. Opposite our house lived an old artist who worked also for the illustrated papers for a living, but painted landscapes for his pleasure, and of him I remember nothing except that he had outlived ambition, was a good listener, and that my father explained his gaunt appearance by his descent from Pocahontas. If all these men were a little like becalmed ships, there was certainly one man whose sails were full. Three or four doors off, on our side of the road, lived a decorative artist in all the naive confidence of popular ideals and the public approval. He was our daily comedy. 'I myself and Sir Frederick Leighton are the greatest decorative artists of the age,' was among his sayings, & a great lych-gate, bought from some country church-yard, reared its thatched roof, meant to shelter bearers and coffin, above the entrance to his front garden, to show that he at any rate knew nothing of discouragement. In this fairly numerous company, there were others though no other face rises before me, my father and York Powell found listeners for a conversation that had no special loyalties, or antagonisms; while I could only talk upon set topics, being in the heat of my youth, and the topics that filled me with excitement were never spoken of.

IV

Some quarter of an hour's walk from Bedford Park, out on the high road to Richmond, lived W. E. Henley, and I, like many others, began under him my education. His portrait, a lithograph by Rothenstein, hangs over my mantlepiece among portraits of other friends. He is drawn standing, but, because doubtless of his crippled legs, he leans forward, resting his elbows upon some slightly suggested object, a table or a window-sill. His heavy figure and powerful head, the disordered hair standing upright, his short irregular beard and moustache, his lined and wrinkled face, his eyes steadily fixed upon some object, in complete confidence and self-possession, and yet as in half-broken reverie, all are exactly as I remember him. I have seen other portraits and they too show him exactly as I remember him, as though he had but one appearance and that seen fully at the first glance and by all alike. He was most human, human, I used to say, like one of Shakespeare's characters, and yet pressed and pummelled, as it were, into a single attitude, almost into a gesture and a speech, as by some overwhelming situation. I disagreed with him about everything, but I admired him beyond words. With the exception of some early poems founded upon old French models, I disliked his poetry, mainly because he wrote Vers Libre, which I associated with Tyndall and Huxley and Bastien-Lepage's clownish peasant staring with vacant eyes at her great boots; and filled it with unimpassioned description of an hospital ward where his leg had been amputated. I wanted the strongest passions, passions that had nothing to do with observation, and metrical forms that seemed old enough to be sung by men half-asleep or riding upon a journey. Furthermore, Pre-Raphaelitism affected him as some people are affected by a cat in the room, and though he professed himself at our first meeting without political interests or convictions, he soon grew into a violent unionist and imperialist. I used to say when I spoke of his poems: 'He is like a great actor with a bad part; yet who would look at Hamlet in the grave scene if Salvini played the grave-digger?' and I might so have explained much that he said and did. I meant that he was like a great actor of passion, character-acting meant nothing to me for many years, and an actor of passion will display someone quality of soul, personified again and again, just as a great poetical painter, Titian, Botticelli, Rossetti may depend for his greatness upon a type of beauty which presently we call by his name. Irving, the last of the sort on the English stage, and in modern England and France it is the rarest sort, never moved me but in the expression of intellectual pride; and though I saw Salvini but once, I am convinced that his genius was a kind of animal nobility. Henley, half inarticulate, 'I am very costive,' he would say, beset with personal quarrels, built up an image of power and magnanimity till it became, at moments, when seen as it were by lightning, his true self. Half his opinions were the contrivance of a sub-consciousness that sought always to bring life to the dramatic crisis, and expression to that point of artifice where the true self could find its tongue. Without opponents there had been no drama, and in his youth Ruskinism and Pre-Raphaelitism, for he was of my father's generation, were the only possible opponents. How could one resent his prejudice when, that he himself might play a worthy part, he must find beyond the common rout, whom he derided and flouted daily, opponents he could imagine moulded like himself? Once he said to me in the height of his imperial propaganda, 'Tell those young men in Ireland that this great thing must go on. They say Ireland is not fit for self-government but that is nonsense. It is as fit as any other European country but we cannot grant it.' And then he spoke of his desire to found and edit a Dublin newspaper. It would have expounded the Gaelic propaganda then beginning, though Dr. Hyde had as yet no league, our old stories, our modern literature, everything that did not demand any shred or patch of government. He dreamed of a tyranny but it was that of Cosimo de Medici.

V

We gathered on Sunday evenings in two rooms, with folding doors between, & hung, I think, with photographs from Dutch masters, and in one room there was always, I think, a table with cold meat. I can recall but one elderly man, Dunn his name was, rather silent and full of good sense, an old friend of Henley's. We were young men, none as yet established in his own, or in the world's opinion, and Henley was our leader and our confidant. One evening I found him alone amused and exasperated.

He cried: 'Young A... has just been round to ask my advice. Would I think it a wise thing if he bolted with Mrs. B...? "Have you quite determined to do it?" I asked him. "Quite." "Well," I said, "in that case I refuse to give you any advice."' Mrs. B... was a beautiful talented woman, who, as the Welsh triad said of Guinevere, 'was much given to being carried off.' I think we listened to him, and often obeyed him, partly because he was quite plainly not upon the side of our parents. We might have a different ground of quarrel, but the result seemed more important than the ground, and his confident manner and speech made us believe, perhaps for the first time, in victory. And besides, if he did denounce, and in my case he certainly did, what we held in secret reverence, he never failed to associate it with things, or persons, that did not move us to reverence. Once I found him just returned from some art congress in Liverpool or in Manchester. 'The Salvation Armyism of art,' he called it, & gave a grotesque description of some city councillor he had found admiring Turner. Henley, who hated all that Ruskin praised, thereupon derided Turner, and finding the city councillor the next day on the other side of the gallery, admiring some Pre-Raphaelite there, derided that Pre-Raphaelite. The third day Henley discovered the poor man on a chair in the middle of the room, staring disconsolately upon the floor. He terrified us also, and certainly I did not dare, and I think none of us dared, to speak our admiration for book or picture he condemned, but he made us feel always our importance, and no man among us could do good work, or show the promise of it, and lack his praise.

I can remember meeting of a Sunday night Charles Whibley, Kenneth Grahame, author of 'The Golden Age,' Barry Pain, now a well known novelist, R. A. M. Stevenson, art critic and a famous talker, George Wyndham, later on a cabinet minister and Irish chief secretary, and Oscar Wilde, who was some eight years or ten older than the rest. But faces and names are vague to me and, while faces that I met but once may rise clearly before me, a face met on many a Sunday has perhaps vanished. Kipling came sometimes, I think, but I never met him; and Stepniak, the nihilist, whom I knew well elsewhere but not there, said 'I cannot go more than once a year, it is too exhausting.' Henley got the best out of us all, because he had made us accept him as our judge and we knew that his judgment could neither sleep, nor be softened, nor changed, nor turned aside. When I think of him, the antithesis that is the foundation of human nature being ever in my sight, I see his crippled legs as though he were some Vulcan perpetually forging swords for other men to use; and certainly I always thought of C..., a fine classical scholar, a pale and seemingly gentle man, as our chief swordsman and bravo. When Henley founded his weekly newspaper, first the 'Scots,' afterwards 'The National Observer,' this young man wrote articles and reviews notorious for savage wit; and years afterwards when 'The National Observer' was dead, Henley dying & our cavern of outlaws empty, I met him in Paris very sad and I think very poor. 'Nobody will employ me now,' he said. 'Your master is gone,' I answered, 'and you are like the spear in an old Irish story that had to be kept dipped in poppy- juice that it might not go about killing people on its own account.' I wrote my first good lyrics and tolerable essays for 'The National Observer' and as I always signed my work could go my own road in some measure. Henley often revised my lyrics, crossing out a line or a stanza and writing in one of his own, and I was comforted by my belief that he also re-wrote Kipling then in the first flood of popularity. At first, indeed, I was ashamed of being re-written and thought that others were not, and only began investigation when the editorial characteristics, epigrams, archaisms and all, appeared in the article upon Paris fashions and in that upon opium by an Egyptian Pasha. I was not compelled to full conformity for verse is plainly stubborn; and in prose, that I might avoid unacceptable opinions, I wrote nothing but ghost or fairy stories, picked up from my mother, or some pilot at Rosses Point, and Henley saw that I must needs mix a palette fitted to my subject matter. But if he had changed every 'has' into 'hath' I would have let him, for had not we sunned ourselves in his generosity? 'My young men out-dome and they write better than I,' he wrote in some letter praising Charles Whibley's work, and to another friend with a copy of my 'Man who dreamed of Fairyland:' 'See what a fine thing has been written by one of my lads.'

VI

My first meeting with Oscar Wilde was an astonishment. I never before heard a man talking with perfect sentences, as if he had written them all over night with labour and yet all spontaneous. There was present that night at Henley's, by right of propinquity or of accident, a man full of the secret spite of dullness, who interrupted from time to time and always to check or disorder thought; and I noticed with what mastery he was foiled and thrown. I noticed, too, that the impression of artificiality that I think all Wilde's listeners have recorded, came from the perfect rounding of the sentences and from the deliberation that made it possible. That very impression helped him as the effect of metre, or of the antithetical prose of the seventeenth century, which is itself a true metre, helps a writer, for he could pass without incongruity from some unforeseen swift stroke of wit to elaborate reverie. I heard him say a few nights later: 'Give me "The Winter's Tale," "Daffodils that come before the swallow dare" but not "King Lear." What is "King Lear" but poor life staggering in the fog?' and the slow cadence, modulated with so great precision, sounded natural to my ears. That first night he praised Walter Pater's 'Essays on the Renaissance:' 'It is my golden book; I never travel anywhere without it; but it is the very flower of decadence. The last trumpet should have sounded the moment it was written.' 'But,' said the dull man, 'would you not have given us time to read it?' 'Oh no,' was the retort, 'there would have been plenty of time afterwards, in either world.' I think he seemed to us, baffled as we were by youth, or by infirmity, a triumphant figure, and to some of us a figure from another age, an audacious Italian fifteenth century figure. A few weeks before I had heard one of my father's friends, an official in a publishing firm that had employed both Wilde and Henley as editors, blaming Henley who was 'no use except under control' and praising Wilde, 'so indolent but such a genius;' and now the firm became the topic of our talk. 'How often do you go to the office?' said Henley. 'I used to go three times a week,' said Wilde, 'for an hour a day but I have since struck off one of the days.' 'My God,' said Henley, 'I went five times a week for five hours a day and when I wanted to strike off a day they had a special committee meeting.' 'Furthermore,' was Wilde's answer, 'I never answered their letters. I have known men come to London full of bright prospects and seen them complete wrecks in a few months through a habit of answering letters.' He too knew how to keep our elders in their place, and his method was plainly the more successful for Henley had been dismissed. 'No he is not an aesthete,' Henley commented later, being somewhat embarrassed by Wilde's Pre-Raphaelite entanglement. 'One soon finds that he is a scholar and a gentleman.' And when I dined with Wilde a few days afterwards he began at once, 'I had to strain every nerve to equal that man at all;' and I was too loyal to speak my thought: 'You & not he' said all the brilliant things. He like the rest of us had felt the strain of an intensity that seemed to hold life at the point of drama. He had said, on that first meeting, 'The basis of literary friendship is mixing the poisoned bowl;' and for a few weeks Henley and he became close friends till, the astonishment of their meeting over, diversity of character and ambition pushed them apart, and, with half the cavern helping, Henley began mixing the poisoned bowl for Wilde. Yet Henley never wholly lost that first admiration, for after Wilde's downfall he said to me: 'Why did he do it? I told my lads to attack him and yet we might have fought under his banner.'

VII

It became the custom, both at Henley's and at Bedford Park, to say that R. A. M. Stevenson, who frequented both circles, was the better talker. Wilde had been trussed up like a turkey by undergraduates, dragged up and down a hill, his champagne emptied into the ice tub, hooted in the streets of various towns and I think stoned, and no newspaper named him but in scorn; his manner had hardened to meet opposition and at times he allowed one to see an unpardonable insolence. His charm was acquired and systematised, a mask which he wore only when it pleased him, while the charm of Stevenson belonged to him like the colour of his hair. If Stevenson's talk became monologue we did not know it, because our one object was to show by our attention that he need never leave off. If thought failed him we would not combat what he had said, or start some new theme, but would encourage him with a question; and one felt that it had been always so from childhood up. His mind was full of phantasy for phantasy's sake and he gave as good entertainment in monologue as his cousin Robert Louis in poem or story. He was always 'supposing:' 'Suppose you had two millions what would you do with it?' and 'Suppose you were in Spain and in love how would you propose?' I recall him one afternoon at our house at Bedford Park, surrounded by my brother and sisters and a little group of my father's friends, describing proposals in half a dozen countries. There your father did it, dressed in such and such a way with such and such words, and there a friend must wait for the lady outside the chapel door, sprinkle her with holy water and say 'My friend Jones is dying for love of you.' But when it was over, those quaint descriptions, so full of laughter and sympathy, faded or remained in the memory as something alien from one's own life like a dance I once saw in a great house, where beautifully dressed children wound a long ribbon in and out as they danced. I was not of Stevenson's party and mainly I think because he had written a book in praise of Velasquez, praise at that time universal wherever Pre-Raphaelitism was accurst, and to my mind, that had to pick its symbols where its ignorance permitted, Velasquez seemed the first bored celebrant of boredom. I was convinced, from some obscure meditation, that Stevenson's conversational method had joined him to my elders and to the indifferent world, as though it were right for old men, and unambitious men and all women, to be content with charm and humour. It was the prerogative of youth to take sides and when Wilde said: 'Mr. Bernard Shaw has no enemies but is intensely disliked by all his friends,' I knew it to be a phrase I should never forget, and felt revenged upon a notorious hater of romance, whose generosity and courage I could not fathom.

VIII

I saw a good deal of Wilde at that time, was it 1887 or 1888? I have no way of fixing the date except that I had published my first book 'The Wanderings of Usheen' and that Wilde had not yet published his 'Decay of Lying.' He had, before our first meeting, reviewed my book and despite its vagueness of intention, and the inexactness of its speech, praised without qualification; and what was worth more than any review had talked about it, and now he asked me to eat my Xmas dinner with him, believing, I imagine, that I was alone in London.

He had just renounced his velveteen, and even those cuffs turned backward over the sleeves, and had begun to dress very carefully in the fashion of the moment. He lived in a little house at Chelsea that the architect Godwin had decorated with an elegance that owed something to Whistler. There was nothing mediaeval, nor Pre-Raphaelite, no cupboard door with figures upon flat gold, no peacock blue, no dark background. I remember vaguely a white drawing room with Whistler etchings, 'let in' to white panels, and a dining room all white: chairs, walls, mantlepiece, carpet, except for a diamond-shaped piece of red cloth in the middle of the table under a terra cotta statuette, and I think a red shaded lamp hanging from the ceiling to a little above the statuette. It was perhaps too perfect in its unity, his past of a few years before had gone too completely, and I remember thinking that the perfect harmony of his life there, with his beautiful wife and his two young children, suggested some deliberate artistic composition.

He commended, & dispraised himself, during dinner by attributing characteristics like his own to his country: 'We Irish are too poetical to be poets; we are a nation of brilliant failures, but we are the greatest talkers since the Greeks.' When dinner was over he read me from the proofs of 'The Decay of Lying' and when he came to the sentence: 'Schopenhauer has analysed the pessimism that characterises modern thought, but Hamlet invented it. The world has become sad because a puppet was once melancholy,' I said, 'Why do you change "sad" to "melancholy?"' He replied that he wanted a full sound at the close of his sentence, and I thought it no excuse and an example of the vague impressiveness that spoilt his writing for me. Only when he spoke, or when his writing was the mirror of his speech, or in some simple fairytale, had he words exact enough to hold a subtle ear. He alarmed me, though not as Henley did for I never left his house thinking myself fool or dunce. He flattered the intellect of every man he liked; he made me tell him long Irish stories and compared my art of story-telling to Homer's; and once when he had described himself as writing in the census paper 'age 19, profession genius, infirmity talent,' the other guest, a young journalist fresh from Oxford or Cambridge, said 'What should I have written?' and was told that it should have been 'profession talent, infirmity genius.' When, however, I called, wearing shoes a little too yellow, unblackened leather had just become fashionable, I understood their extravegence when I saw his eyes fixed upon them; an another day Wilde asked me to tell his little boy a fairy story, and I had but got as far as 'Once upon a time there was a giant' when the little boy screamed and ran out of the room. Wilde looked grave and I was plunged into the shame of clumsiness that afflicts the young. When I asked for some literary gossip for some provincial newspaper, that paid me a few shillings a month, he explained very explicitly that writing literary gossip was no job for a gentleman. Though to be compared to Homer passed the time pleasantly, I had not been greatly perturbed had he stopped me with 'Is it a long story?' as Henley would certainly have done. I was abashed before him as wit and man of the world alone. I remember that he deprecated the very general belief in his success or his efficiency, and I think with sincerity. One form of success had gone: he was no more the lion of the season, and he had not discovered his gift for writing comedy, yet I think I knew him at the happiest moment of his life. No scandal had darkened his fame, his fame as a talker was growing among his equals, & he seemed to live in the enjoyment of his own spontaneity. One day he began: 'I have been inventing a Christian heresy,' and he told a detailed story, in the style of some early father, of how Christ recovered after the Crucifixion and, escaping from the tomb, lived on for many years, the one man upon earth who knew the falsehood of Christianity. Once St. Paul visited his town and he alone in the carpenters' quarter did not go to hear him preach. The other carpenters noticed that henceforth, for some unknown reason, he kept his hands covered. A few days afterwards I found Wilde, with smock frocks in various colours spread out upon the floor in front of him, while a missionary explained that he did not object to the heathen going naked upon week days, but insisted upon clothes in church. He had brought the smock frocks in a cab that the only art-critic whose fame had reached Central Africa might select a colour; so Wilde sat there weighing all with a conscious ecclesiastic solemnity.

IX

Of late years I have often explained Wilde to myself by his family history. His father, was a friend or acquaintance of my father's father and among my family traditions there is an old Dublin riddle: 'Why are Sir William Wilde's nails so black?' Answer, 'Because he has scratched himself.' And there is an old story still current in Dublin of Lady Wilde saying to a servant. 'Why do you put the plates on the coal-scuttle? What are the chairs meant for?' They were famous people and there are many like stories, and even a horrible folk story, the invention of some Connaught peasant, that tells how Sir William Wilde took out the eyes of some men, who had come to consult him as an oculist, and laid them upon a plate, intending to replace them in a moment, and how the eyes were eaten by a cat. As a certain friend of mine, who has made a prolonged study of the nature of cats, said when he first heard the tale, 'Catslove eyes.' The Wilde family was clearly of the sort that fed the imagination of Charles Lever, dirty, untidy, daring, and what Charles Lever, who loved more normal activities, might not have valued so highly, very imaginative and learned. Lady Wilde, who when I knew her received her friends with blinds drawn and shutters closed that none might see her withered face, longed always perhaps, though certainly amid much self mockery, for some impossible splendour of character and circumstance. She lived near her son in level Chelsea, but I have heard her say, 'I want to live on some high place, Primrose Hill or Highgate, because I was an eagle in my youth.' I think her son lived with no self mockery at all an imaginary life; perpetually performed a play which was in all things the opposite of all that he had known in childhood and early youth; never put off completely his wonder at opening his eyes every morning on his own beautiful house, and in remembering that he had dined yesterday with a duchess and that he delighted in Flaubert and Pater, read Homer in the original and not as a school-master reads him for the grammar. I think, too, that because of all that half-civilized blood in his veins, he could not endure the sedentary toil of creative art and so remained a man of action, exaggerating, for the sake of immediate effect, every trick learned from his masters, turning their easel painting into painted scenes. He was a parvenu, but a parvenu whose whole bearing proved that if he did dedicate every story in 'The House of Pomegranates' to a lady of title, it was but to show that he was Jack and the social ladder his pantomime beanstalk. "Did you ever hear him say 'Marquess of Dimmesdale'?" a friend of his once asked me. "He does not say 'the Duke of York' with any pleasure."

He told me once that he had been offered a safe seat in Parliament and, had he accepted, he might have had a career like that of Beaconsfield, whose early style resembles his, being meant for crowds, for excitement, for hurried decisions, for immediate triumphs. Such men get their sincerity, if at all, from the contact of events; the dinner table was Wilde's event and made him the greatest talker of his time, and his plays and dialogues have what merit they possess from being now an imitation, now a record, of his talk. Even in those days I would often defend him by saying that his very admiration for his predecessors in poetry, for Browning, for Swinburne and Rossetti, in their first vogue while he was a very young man, made any success seem impossible that could satisfy his immense ambition: never but once before had the artist seemed so great, never had the work of art seemed so difficult. I would then compare him with Benvenuto Cellini who, coming after Michael Angelo, found nothing left to do so satisfactory as to turn bravo and assassinate the man who broke Michael Angelo's nose.

X

I cannot remember who first brought me to the old stable beside Kelmscott House, William Morris' house at Hammersmith, & to the debates held there upon Sunday evenings by the socialist League. I was soon of the little group who had supper with Morris afterwards. I met at these suppers very constantly Walter Crane, Emery Walker presently, in association with Cobden Sanderson, the printer of many fine books, and less constantly Bernard Shaw and Cockerell, now of the museum of Cambridge, and perhaps but once or twice Hyndman the socialist and the anarchist Prince Krapotkin. There too one always met certain more or less educated workmen, rough of speech and manner, with a conviction to meet every turn. I was told by one of them, on a night when I had done perhaps more than my share of the talking, that I had talked more nonsense in one evening than he had heard in the whole course of his past life. I had merely preferred Parnell, then at the height of his career, to Michael Davitt who had wrecked his Irish influence by international politics. We sat round a long unpolished and unpainted trestle table of new wood in a room where hung Rossetti's 'Pomegranate,' a portrait of Mrs. Morris, and where one wall and part of the ceiling were covered by a great Persian carpet. Morris had said somewhere or other that carpets were meant for people who took their shoes off when they entered a house, and were most in place upon a tent floor. I was a little disappointed in the house, for Morris was an old man content at last to gather beautiful things rather than to arrange a beautiful house. I saw the drawing-room once or twice and there alone all my sense of decoration, founded upon the background of Rossetti's pictures, was satisfied by a big cupboard painted with a scene from Chaucer by Burne Jones, but even there were objects, perhaps a chair or a little table, that seemed accidental, bought hurriedly perhaps, and with little thought, to make wife or daughter comfortable. I had read as a boy in books belonging to my father, the third volume of 'The Earthly Paradise' and 'The Defence of Guinevere,' which pleased me less, but had not opened either for a long time. 'The man who never laughed again' had seemed the most wonderful of tales till my father had accused me of preferring Morris to Keats, got angry about it and put me altogether out of countenance. He had spoiled my pleasure, for now I questioned while I read and at last ceased to read; nor had Morris written as yet those prose romances that became, after his death, so great a joy that they were the only books I was ever to read slowly that I might not come too quickly to the end. It was now Morris himself that stirred my interest, and I took to him first because of some little tricks of speech and body that reminded me of my old grandfather in Sligo, but soon discovered his spontaneity and joy and made him my chief of men. To-day I do not set his poetry very high, but for an odd altogether wonderful line, or thought; and yet, if some angel offered me the choice, I would choose to live his life, poetry and all, rather than my own or any other man's. A reproduction of his portrait by Watts hangs over my mantlepiece with Henley's, and those of other friends. Its grave wide-open eyes, like the eyes of some dreaming beast, remind me of the open eyes of Titian's' Ariosto,' while the broad vigorous body suggests a mind that has no need of the intellect to remain sane, though it give itself to every phantasy, the dreamer of the middle ages. It is 'the fool of fairy ... wide and wild as a hill,' the resolute European image that yet half remembers Buddha's motionless meditation, and has no trait in common with the wavering, lean image of hungry speculation, that cannot but fill the mind's eye because of certain famous Hamlets of our stage. Shakespeare himself foreshadowed a symbolic change, that shows a change in the whole temperament of the world, for though he called his Hamlet 'fat, and scant of breath,' he thrust between his fingers agile rapier and dagger.

The dream world of Morris was as much the antithesis of daily life as with other men of genius, but he was never conscious of the antithesis and so knew nothing of intellectual suffering. His intellect, unexhausted by speculation or casuistry, was wholly at the service of hand and eye, and whatever he pleased he did with an unheard of ease and simplicity, and if style and vocabulary were at times monotonous, he could not have made them otherwise without ceasing to be himself. Instead of the language of Chaucer and Shakespeare, its warp fresh from field and market, if the woof were learned, his age offered him a speech, exhausted from abstraction, that only returned to its full vitality when written learnedly and slowly. The roots of his antithetical dream were visible enough: a never idle man of great physical strength and extremely irascible, did he not fling a badly baked plum pudding through the window upon Xmas Day? a man more joyous than any intellectual man of our world, called himself 'the idle singer of an empty day' created new forms of melancholy, and faint persons, like the knights & ladies of Burne Jones, who are never, no, not once in forty volumes, put out of temper. A blunderer, who had said to the only unconverted man at a socialist picnic in Dublin, to prove that equality came easy, 'I was brought up a gentleman and now, as you can see, associate with all sorts,' and left wounds thereby that rankled after twenty years, a man of whom I have heard it said 'He is always afraid that he is doing something wrong, and generally is,' wrote long stories with apparently no other object than that his persons might show one another, through situations of poignant difficulty, the most exquisite tact.

He did not project, like Henley or like Wilde, an image of himself, because, having all his imagination set on making and doing, he had little self-knowledge. He imagined instead new conditions of making and doing; and, in the teeth of those scientific generalisations that cowed my boyhood, I can see some like imagining in every great change, believing that the first flying fish leaped, not because it sought 'adaptation' to the air, but out of horror of the sea.

XI

Soon after I began to attend the lectures, a French class was started in the old coach-house for certain young socialists who planned a tour in France, and I joined it and was for a time a model student constantly encouraged by the compliments of the old French mistress. I told my father of the class, and he asked me to get my sisters admitted. I made difficulties and put off speaking of the matter, for I knew that the new and admirable self I was making would turn, under family eyes, into plain rag doll. How could I pretend to be industrious, and even carry dramatization to the point of learning my lessons, when my sisters were there and knew that I was nothing of the kind? But I had no argument I could use and my sisters were admitted. They said nothing unkind, so far as I can remember, but in a week or two I was my old procrastinating idle self and had soon left the class altogether. My elder sister stayed on and became an embroideress under Miss May Morris, and the hangings round Morris's big bed at Kelmscott House, Oxfordshire, with their verses about lying happily in bed when 'all birds sing in the town of the tree,' were from her needle though not from her design. She worked for the first few months at Kelmscott House, Hammersmith, and in my imagination I cannot always separate what I saw and heard from her report, or indeed from the report of that tribe or guild who looked up to Morris as to some worshipped mediaeval king. He had no need for other people. I doubt if their marriage or death made him sad or glad, and yet no man I have known was so well loved; you saw him producing everywhere organisation and beauty, seeming, almost in the same instant, helpless and triumphant; and people loved him as children are loved. People much in his neighbourhood became gradually occupied with him, or about his affairs, and without any wish on his part, as simple people become occupied with children. I remember a man who was proud and pleased because he had distracted Morris' thoughts from an attack of gout by leading the conversation delicately to the hated name of Milton. He began at Swinburne. 'Oh, Swinburne,' said Morris, 'is a rhetorician; my masters have been Keats and Chaucer for they make pictures.' 'Does not Milton make pictures?' asked my informant. 'No,' was the answer, 'Dante makes pictures, but Milton, though he had a great earnest mind, expressed himself as a rhetorician.' 'Great earnest mind,' sounded strange to me and I doubt not that were his questioner not a simple man, Morris had been more violent. Another day the same man started by praising Chaucer, but the gout was worse and Morris cursed Chaucer for destroying the English language with foreign words.

He had few detachable phrases and I can remember little of his speech, which many thought the best of all good talk, except that it matched his burly body and seemed within definite boundaries inexhaustible in fact and expression. He alone of all the men I have known seemed guided by some beast-like instinct and never ate strange meat. 'Balzac! Balzac!' he said to me once, 'Oh, that was the man the French bourgeoisie read so much a few years ago.' I can remember him at supper praising wine: 'Why do people say it is prosaic to be inspired by wine? Has it not been made by the sunlight and the sap?' and his dispraising houses decorated by himself: 'Do you suppose I like that kind of house? I would like a house like a big barn, where one ate in one corner, cooked in another corner, slept in the third corner & in the fourth received one's friends'; and his complaining of Ruskin's objection to the underground railway: 'If you must have a railway the best thing you can do with it is to put it in a tube with a cork at each end.' I remember too that when I asked what led up to his movement, he replied, 'Oh, Ruskin and Carlyle, but somebody should have been beside Carlyle and punched his head every five minutes.' Though I remember little, I do not doubt that, had I continued going there on Sunday evenings, I should have caught fire from his words and turned my hand to some mediaeval work or other. Just before I had ceased to go there I had sent my 'Wanderings of Usheen' to his daughter, hoping of course that it might meet his eyes, & soon after sending it I came upon him by chance in Holborn. 'You write my sort of poetry,' he said and began to praise me and to promise to send his praise to 'The Commonwealth,' the League organ, and he would have said more of a certainty had he not caught sight of a new ornamental cast-iron lamp-post and got very heated upon that subject.

I did not read economics, having turned socialist because of Morris's lectures and pamphlets, and I think it unlikely that Morris himself could read economics. That old dogma of mine seemed germane to the matter. If the men and women imagined by the poets were the norm, and if Morris had, in, let us say, 'News from Nowhere,' then running through 'The Commonwealth,' described such men and women living under their natural conditions or as they would desire to live, then those conditions themselves must be the norm, and could we but get rid of certain institutions the world would turn from eccentricity. Perhaps Morris himself justified himself in his own heart by as simple an argument, and was, as the socialist D... said to me one night walking home after some lecture, 'an anarchist without knowing it.' Certainly I and all about me, including D... himself, were for chopping up the old king for Medea's pot. Morris had told us to have nothing to do with the parliamentary socialists, represented for men in general by the Fabian Society and Hyndman's Socialist Democratic Federation and for us in particular by D... During the period of transition mistakes must be made, and the discredit of these mistakes must be left to 'the bourgeoisie;' and besides, when you begin to talk of this measure or that other you lose sight of the goal and see, to reverse Swinburne's description of Tiresias, 'light on the way but darkness on the goal.' By mistakes Morris meant vexatious restrictions and compromises, 'If any man puts me into a labour squad, I will lie on my back and kick.' That phrase very much expresses our idea of revolutionary tactics: we all intended to lie upon our back and kick. D..., pale and sedentary, did not dislike labour squads and we all hated him with the left side of our heads, while admiring him immensely with the right. He alone was invited to entertain Mrs. Morris, having many tales of his Irish uncles, more especially of one particular uncle who had tried to commit suicide by shutting his head into a carpet bag. At that time he was an obscure man, known only for a witty speaker at street corners and in Park demonstrations. He had, with an assumed truculence and fury, cold logic, an universal gentleness, an unruffled courtesy, and yet could never close a speech without being denounced by a journeyman hatter with an Italian name. Converted to socialism by D..., and to anarchism by himself, with swinging arm and uplifted voice this man perhaps exaggerated our scruple about parliament. 'I lack,' said D..., 'the bump of reverence;' whereon the wild man shouted 'You 'ave a 'ole.' There are moments when looking back I somewhat confuse my own figure with that of the hatter, image of our hysteria, for I too became violent with the violent solemnity of a religious devotee. I can even remember sitting behind D... and saying some rude thing or other over his shoulder. I don't remember why I gave it up but I did quite suddenly; and I think the push may have come from a young workman who was educating himself between Morris and Karl Marx. He had planned a history of the navy and when I had spoken of the battleship of Nelson's day, had said: 'Oh, that was the decadence of the battleship,' but if his naval interests were mediaeval, his ideas about religion were pure Karl Marx, and we were soon in perpetual argument. Then gradually the attitude towards religion of almost everybody but Morris, who avoided the subject altogether, got upon my nerves, for I broke out after some lecture or other with all the arrogance of raging youth. They attacked religion, I said, or some such words, and yet there must be a change of heart and only religion could make it. What was the use of talking about some near revolution putting all things right, when the change must come, if come it did, with astronomical slowness, like the cooling of the sun or, it may have been, like the drying of the moon? Morris rang his chairman's bell, but I was too angry to listen, and he had to ring it a second time before I sat down. He said that night at supper: 'Of course I know there must be a change of heart, but it will not come as slowly as all that. I rang my bell because you were not being understood.' He did not show any vexation, but I never returned after that night; and yet I did not always believe what I had said and only gradually gave up thinking of and planning for some near sudden change for the better.

XII

I spent my days at the British Museum and must, I think, have been delicate, for I remember often putting off hour after hour after consulting some necessary book because I shrank from lifting the heavy volumes of the catalogue; and yet to save money for my afternoon coffee and roll I often walked the whole way home to Bedford Park. I was compiling, for a series of shilling books, an anthology of Irish fairy stories and, for an American publisher, a two volume selection from the Irish novelists that would be somewhat dearer. I was not well paid, for each book cost me more than three months' reading; and I was paid for the first some twelve pounds, ('O Mr. E...' said publisher to editor, 'you must never again pay so much') and for the second, twenty; but I did not think myself badly paid, for I had chosen the work for my own purposes.

Though I went to Sligo every summer, I was compelled to live out of Ireland the greater part of every year and was but keeping my mind upon what I knew must be the subject matter of my poetry. I believed that if Morris had set his stories amid the scenery of his own Wales (for I knew him to be of Welsh extraction and supposed wrongly that he had spent his childhood there) that if Shelley had nailed his Prometheus or some equal symbol upon some Welsh or Scottish rock, their art had entered more intimately, more microscopically, as it were, into our thought, and had given perhaps to modern poetry a breadth and stability like that of ancient poetry. The statues of Mausolus and

Artemisia at the British Museum, private, half animal, half divine figures, all unlike the Grecian athletes and Egyptian kings in their near neighbourhood, that stand in the middle of the crowd's applause or sit above measuring it out unpersuadable justice, became to me, now or later, images of an unpremeditated joyous energy, that neither I nor any other man, racked by doubt and enquiry, can achieve; and that yet, if once achieved, might seem to men and women of Connemara or of Galway their very soul. In our study of that ruined tomb, raised by a queen to her dead lover, and finished by the unpaid labour of great sculptors after her death from grief, or so runs the tale, we cannot distinguish the handiworks of Scopas and Praxiteles; and I wanted to create once more an art, where the artist's handiwork would hide as under those half anonymous chisels, or as we find it in some old Scots ballads or in some twelfth or thirteenth century Arthurian romance. That handiwork assured, I had martyred no man for modelling his own image upon Pallas Athena's buckler; for I took great pleasure in certain allusions to the singer's life one finds in old romances and ballads, and thought his presence there all the more poignant because we discover it half lost, like portly Chaucer riding behind his Maunciple and his Pardoner. Wolfram von Eschenbach, singing his German Parsival, broke off some description of a famished city to remember that in his own house at home the very mice lacked food, and what old ballad singer was it who claimed to have fought by day in the very battle he sang by night? So masterful indeed was that instinct that when the minstrel knew not who his poet was he must needs make up a man: 'When any stranger asks who is the sweetest of singers, answer with one voice: "A blind man; he dwells upon rocky Chios; his songs shall be the most beautiful forever."' Elaborate modern psychology sounds egotistical, I thought, when it speaks in the first person, but not those simple emotions which resemble the more, the more powerful they are, everybody's emotion, and I was soon to write many poems where an always personal emotion was woven into a general pattern of myth and symbol. When the Fenian poet says that his heart has grown cold and callous, 'For thy hapless fate, dear Ireland, and sorrows of my own,' he but follows tradition, and if he does not move us deeply, it is because he has no sensuous musical vocabulary that comes at need, without compelling him to sedentary toil and so driving him out from his fellows. I thought to create that sensuous, musical vocabulary, and not for myself only but that I might leave it to later Irish poets, much as a mediaeval Japanese painter left his style as an inheritance to his family, and was careful to use a traditional manner and matter; yet did something altogether different, changed by that toil, impelled by my share in Cain's curse, by all that sterile modern complication, by my 'originality' as the newspapers call it. Morris set out to make a revolution that the persons of his 'Well at the World's End' or his 'Waters of the Wondrous Isles,' always, to my mind, in the likeness of Artemisia and her man, might walk his native scenery; and I, that my native scenery might find imaginary inhabitants, half planned a new method and a new culture. My mind began drifting vaguely towards that doctrine of 'the mask' which has convinced me that every passionate man (I have nothing to do with mechanist, or philanthropist, or man whose eyes have no preference) is, as it were, linked with another age, historical or imaginary, where alone he finds images that rouse his energy. Napoleon was never of his own time, as the naturalistic writers and painters bid all men be, but had some Roman Emperor's image in his head and some condottiere's blood in his heart; and when he crowned that head at Rome with his own hands, he had covered, as may be seen from David's painting, his hesitation with that Emperor's old suit.

XIII

I had various women friends on whom I would call towards five o'clock, mainly to discuss my thoughts that I could not bring to a man without meeting some competing thought, but partly because their tea & toast saved my pennies for the 'bus ride home; but with women, apart from their intimate exchanges of thought, I was timid and abashed. I was sitting on a seat in front of the British Museum feeding pigeons, when a couple of girls sat near and began enticing my pigeons away, laughing and whispering to one another, and I looked straight in front of me, very indignant, and presently went into the Museum without turning my head towards them. Since then I have often wondered if they were pretty or merely very young. Sometimes I told myself very adventurous love stories with myself for hero, and at other times I planned out a life of lonely austerity, and at other times mixed the ideals and planned a life of lonely austerity mitigated by periodical lapses. I had still the ambition, formed in Sligo in my teens, of living in imitation of Thoreau on Innisfree, a little island in Lough Gill, and when walking through Fleet Street very homesick I heard a little tinkle of water and saw a fountain in a shop window which balanced a little ball upon its jet and began to remember lake water. From the sudden remembrance came my poem 'Innisfree,' my first lyric with anything in its rhythm of my own music. I had begun to loosen rhythm as an escape from rhetoric, and from that emotion of the crowd that rhetoric brings, but I only understood vaguely and occasionally that I must, for my special purpose, use nothing but the common syntax. A couple of years later I would not have written that first line with its conventional archaism, 'Arise and go', nor the inversion in the last stanza. Passing another day by the new Law Courts, a building that I admired because it was Gothic,, 'It is not very good,' Morris had said, 'but it is better than anything else they have got and so they hate it.' I grew suddenly oppressed by the great weight of stone, and thought, 'There are miles and miles of stone and brick all round me,' and presently added, 'If John the Baptist, or his like, were to come again and had his mind set upon it, he could make all these people go out into some wilderness leaving their buildings empty,' and that thought, which does not seem very valuable now, so enlightened the day that it is still vivid in the memory. I spent a few days at Oxford copying out a seventeenth century translation of Poggio's Liber Facetiarum or the Hypneroto-machia of Poliphili for a publisher; I forget which, for I copied both; and returned very pale to my troubled family. I had lived upon bread and tea because I thought that if antiquity found locust and wild honey nutritive, my soul was strong enough to need no better. I was always planning some great gesture, putting the whole world into one scale of the balance and my soul into the other, and imagining that the whole world somehow kicked the beam. More than thirty years have passed and I have seen no forcible young man of letters brave the metropolis without some like stimulant; and all, after two or three, or twelve or fifteen years, according to obstinacy, have understood that we achieve, if we do achieve, in little diligent sedentary stitches as though we were making lace. I had one unmeasured advantage from my stimulant: I could ink my socks, that they might not show through my shoes, with a most haughty mind, imagining myself, and my torn tackle, somewhere else, in some far place 'under the canopy ... i' the city of kites and crows.'

In London I saw nothing good, and constantly remembered that Ruskin had said to some friend of my father's, 'As I go to my work at the British Museum I see the faces of the people become daily more corrupt.' I convinced myself for a time, that on the same journey I saw but what he saw. Certain old women's faces filled me with horror, faces that are no longer there, or if they are, pass before me unnoticed: the fat blotched faces, rising above double chins, of women who have drunk too much beer and eaten too much meat. In Dublin I had often seen old women walking with erect heads and gaunt bodies, talking to themselves in loud voices, mad with drink and poverty, but they were different, they belonged to romance: Da Vinci has drawn women who looked so and so carried their bodies.

XIV

I attempted to restore one old friend of my father's to the practice of his youth, but failed though he, unlike my father, had not changed his belief. My father brought me to dine with Jack Nettleship at Wigmore Street, once inventor of imaginative designs and now a painter of melodramatic lions. At dinner I had talked a great deal, too much, I imagine, for so young a man, or may be for any man, and on the way home my father, who had been plainly anxious that I should make a good impression, was very angry. He said I had talked for effect and that talking for effect was precisely what one must never do; he had always hated rhetoric and emphasis and had made me hate it; and his anger plunged me into great dejection. I called at Nettleship's studio the next day to apologise and Nettleship opened the door himself and received me with enthusiasm. He had explained to some woman guest that I would probably talk well, being an Irishman, but the reality had surpassed, etc., etc. I was not flattered, though relieved at not having to apologise, for I soon discovered that what he really admired was my volubility, for he himself was very silent. He seemed about sixty, had a bald head, a grey beard, and a nose, as one of my father's friends used to say, like an opera glass, and sipped cocoa all the afternoon and evening from an enormous tea cup that must have been designed for him alone, not caring how cold the cocoa grew. Years before he had been thrown from his horse while hunting and broken his arm and, because it had been badly set, suffered great pain for along time. A little whiskey would always stop the pain, and soon a little became a great deal and he found himself a drunkard, but having signed his liberty away for certain months he was completely cured. He had acquired, however, the need of some liquid which he could sip constantly. I brought him an admiration settled in early boyhood, for my father had always said, 'George Wilson was our born painter but Nettleship our genius,' and even had he shown me nothing I could care for, I had admired him still because my admiration was in my bones. He showed me his early designs and they, though often badly drawn, fulfilled my hopes. Something of Blake they certainly did show, but had in place of Blake's joyous intellectual energy a Saturnian passion and melancholy. 'God creating evil' the death- like head with a woman and a tiger coming from the forehead, which Rossetti, or was it Browning? had described 'as the most sublime design of ancient or modern art' had been lost, but there was another version of the same thought and other designs never published or exhibited. They rise before me even now in meditation, especially a blind Titan-like ghost floating with groping hands above the treetops. I wrote a criticism, and arranged for reproductions with the editor of an art magazine, but after it was written and accepted the proprietor, lifting what I considered an obsequious caw in the Huxley, Tyndall, Carolus Duran, Bastien-Lepage rookery, insisted upon its rejection. Nettleship did not mind its rejection, saying, 'Who cares for such things now? Not ten people,' but he did mind my refusal to show him what I had written. Though what I had written was all eulogy, I dreaded his judgment for it was my first art criticism. I hated his big lion pictures, where he attempted an art too much concerned with the sense of touch, with the softness or roughness, the minutely observed irregularity of surfaces, for his genius; and I think he knew it. 'Rossetti used to call my pictures 'pot- boilers,' he said, 'but they are all, all,' and he waved his arms to the canvases, 'symbols.' When I wanted him to design gods and angels and lost spirits once more, he always came back to the point, 'Nobody would be pleased.' 'Everybody should have a raison d'etre' was one of his phrases. 'Mrs--'s articles are not good but they are her raison d'etre.' I had but little knowledge of art, for there was little scholarship in the Dublin Art School, so I overrated the quality of anything that could be connected with my general beliefs about the world. If I had been able to give angelical, or diabolical names to his lions I might have liked them also and I think that Nettleship himself would have liked them better, and liking them better have become a better painter. We had the same kind of religious feeling, but I could give a crude philosophical expression to mine while he could only express his in action or with brush and pencil. He often told me of certain ascetic ambitions, very much like my own, for he had kept all the moral ambition of youth with a moral courage peculiar to himself, as for instance, 'Yeats, the other night I was arrested by a policeman, was walking round Regent's Park barefooted to keep the flesh under, good sort of thing to do, I was carrying my boots in my hand and he thought I was a burglar; and even when I explained and gave him half a crown, he would not let me go till I had promised to put on my boots before I met the next policeman.'

He was very proud and shy, and I could not imagine anybody asking him questions, and so I was content to take these stories as they came, confirmations of stories I had heard in boyhood. One story in particular had stirred my imagination, for, ashamed all my boyhood of my lack of physical courage, I admired what was beyond my imitation. He thought that any weakness, even a weakness of body, had the character of sin, and while at breakfast with his brother, with whom he shared a room on the third floor of a corner house, he said that his nerves were out of order. Presently he left the table, and got out through the window and on to a stone ledge that ran along the wall under the windowsills. He sidled along the ledge, and turning the corner with it, got in at a different window and returned to the table. 'My nerves,' he said, 'are better than I thought.'

XV

Nettleship said to me: 'Has Edwin Ellis ever said anything about the effect of drink upon my genius?' 'No,' I answered. 'I ask,' he said, 'because I have always thought that Ellis has some strange medical insight.' Though I had answered 'no,' Ellis had only a few days before used these words: 'Nettleship drank his genius away.' Ellis, but lately returned from Perugia, where he had lived many years, was another old friend of my father's but some years younger than Nettleship or my father. Nettleship had found his simplifying image, but in his painting had turned away from it, while Ellis, the son of Alexander Ellis, a once famous man of science, who was perhaps the last man in England to run the circle of the sciences without superficiality, had never found that image at all. He was a painter and poet, but his painting, which did not interest me, showed no influence but that of Leighton. He had started perhaps a couple of years too late for Pre-Raphaelite influence, for no great Pre-Raphaelite picture was painted after 1870, and left England too soon for that of the French painters. He was, however, sometimes moving as a poet and still more often an astonishment. I have known him cast something just said into a dozen lines of musical verse, without apparently ceasing to talk; but the work once done he could not or would not amend it, and my father thought he lacked all ambition. Yet he had at times nobility of rhythm, an instinct for grandeur, and after thirty years I still repeat to myself his address to Mother Earth:

O mother of the hills, forgive our towers;
O mother of the clouds, forgive our dreams

and there are certain whole poems that I read from time to time or try to make others read. There is that poem where the manner is unworthy of the matter, being loose and facile, describing Adam and Eve fleeing from Paradise. Adam asks Eve what she carries so carefully and Eve replies that it is a little of the apple core kept for their children. There is that vision of 'Christ the Less,' a too hurriedly written ballad, where the half of Christ, sacrificed to the divine half 'that fled to seek felicity,' wanders wailing through Golgotha; and there is 'The Saint and the Youth' in which I can discover no fault at all. He loved complexities, 'seven silences like candles round her face' is a line of his, and whether he wrote well or ill had always a manner, which I would have known from that of any other poet. He would say to me, 'I am a mathematician with the mathematics left out', his father was a great mathematician or 'A woman once said to me, "Mr. Ellis why are your poems like sums?"' and certainly he loved symbols and abstractions. He said once, when I had asked him not to mention something or other, 'Surely you have discovered by this time that I know of no means whereby I can mention a fact in conversation.'

He had a passion for Blake, picked up in Pre-Raphaelite studios, and early in our acquaintance put into my hands a scrap of note paper on which he had written some years before an interpretation of the poem that begins

The fields from Islington to Marylebone
To Primrose Hill and St. John's Wood
Were builded over with pillars of gold
And there Jerusalem's pillars stood.

The four quarters of London represented Blake's four great mythological personages, the Zoas, and also the four elements. These few sentences were the foundation of all study of the philosophy of William Blake, that requires an exact knowledge for its pursuit and that traces the connection between his system and that of Swedenborg or of Boehme. I recognised certain attributions, from what is sometimes called the Christian Cabala, of which Ellis had never heard, and with this proof that his interpretation was more than phantasy, he and I began our four years' work upon the Prophetic Books of William Blake. We took it as almost a sign of Blake's personal help when we discovered that the spring of 1889, when we first joined our knowledge, was one hundred years from the publication of 'The Book of Thel,' the first published of the Prophetic Books, as though it were firmly established that the dead delight in anniversaries. After months of discussion and reading, we made a concordance of all Blake's mystical terms, and there was much copying to be done in the Museum & at Red Hill, where the descendants of Blake's friend and patron, the landscape painter, John Linnell, had many manuscripts. The Linnellswere narrow in their religious ideas & doubtful of Blake's orthodoxy, whom they held, however, in great honour, and I remember a timid old lady who had known Blake when a child saying: 'He had very wrong ideas, he did not believe in the historical Jesus.' One old man sat always beside us ostensibly to sharpen our pencils, but perhaps really to see that we did not steal the manuscripts, and they gave us very old port at lunch and I have upon my dining room walls their present of Blake's Dante engravings. Going thither and returning Ellis would entertain me by philosophical discussion, varied with improvised stories, at first folk tales which he professed to have picked up in Scotland; and though I had read and collected many folk tales, I did not see through the deceit. I have a partial memory of two more elaborate tales, one of an Italian conspirator flying barefoot from I forget what adventure through I forget what Italian city, in the early morning. Fearing to be recognised by his bare feet, he slipped past the sleepy porter at an hotel calling out 'number so and so' as if he were some belated guest. Then passing from bedroom door to door he tried on the boots, and just as he got a pair to fit a voice cried from the room 'Who is that?' 'Merely me, sir,' he called back, 'taking your boots.' The other was of a Martyr's Bible round which the cardinal virtues had taken personal form, this a fragment of Blake's philosophy. It was in the possession of an old clergyman when a certain jockey called upon him, and the cardinal virtues, confused between jockey and clergyman, devoted themselves to the jockey. As whenever he sinned a cardinal virtue interfered and turned him back to virtue, he lived in great credit and made, but for one sentence, a very holy death. As his wife and family knelt round in admiration and grief, he suddenly said 'Damn.' 'O my dear,' said his wife, 'what a dreadful expression.' He answered, 'I am going to heaven' and straightway died. It was a long tale, for there were all the jockey's vain attempts to sin, as well as all the adventures of the clergyman, who became very sinful indeed, but it ended happily, for when the jockey died the cardinal virtues returned to the clergyman. I think he would talk to any audience that offered, one audience being the same as another in his eyes, and it may have been for this reason that my father called him unambitious. When he was a young man he had befriended a reformed thief and had asked the grateful thief to take him round the thieves' quarters of London. The thief, however, hurried him away from the worst saying, 'Another minute and they would have found you out. If they were not the stupidest men in London, they had done so already.' Ellis had gone through a no doubt romantic and witty account of all the houses he had robbed, and all the throats he had cut in one short life.

His conversation would often pass out of my comprehension, or indeed I think of any man's, into a labyrinth of abstraction and subtilty, and then suddenly return with some verbal conceit or turn of wit. The mind is known to attain, in certain conditions of trance, a quickness so extraordinary that we are compelled at times to imagine a condition of unendurable intellectual intensity, from which we are saved by the merciful stupidity of the body; & I think that the mind of Edwin Ellis was constantly upon the edge of trance. Once we were discussing the symbolism of sex, in the philosophy of Blake, and had been in disagreement all the afternoon. I began talking with a new sense of conviction, and after a moment Ellis, who was at his easel, threw down his brush and said that he had just seen the same explanation in a series of symbolic visions. 'In another moment,' he said, 'I should have been off.' We went into the open air and walked up and down to get rid of that feeling, but presently we came in again and I began again my explanation, Ellis lying upon the sofa. I had been talking some time when Mrs. Ellis came into the room and said: 'Why are you sitting in the dark?' Ellis answered, 'But we are not,' and then added in a voice of wonder, 'I thought the lamp was lit and that I was sitting up, and I find I am in the dark and lying down.' I had seen a flicker of light over the ceiling, but had thought it a reflection from some light outside the house, which may have been the case.

XVI

I had already met most of the poets of my generation. I had said, soon after the publication of 'The Wanderings of Usheen,' to the editor of a series of shilling reprints, who had set me to compile tales of the Irish fairies, 'I am growing jealous of other poets, and we will all grow jealous of each other unless we know each other and so feel a share in each other's triumph.' He was a Welshman, lately a mining engineer, Ernest Rhys, a writer of Welsh translations and original poems that have often moved me greatly though I can think of no one else who has read them. He was seven or eight years older than myself and through his work as editor knew everybody who would compile a book for seven or eight pounds. Between us we founded 'The Rhymers' Club' which for some years was to meet every night in an upper room with a sanded floor in an ancient eating house in the Strand called 'The Cheshire Cheese.' Lionel Johnson, Ernest Dowson, Victor Plarr, Ernest Radford, John Davidson, Richard le Gallienne, T. W. Rolleston, Selwyn Image and two men of an older generation, Edwin Ellis and John Todhunter, came constantly for a time, Arthur Symons and Herbert Home less constantly, while William Watson joined but never came and Francis Thompson came once but never joined; and sometimes, if we met in a private house, which we did occasionally, Oscar Wilde came. It had been useless to invite him to the 'Cheshire Cheese' for he hated Bohemia. 'Olive Schreiner,' he said once to me, 'is staying in the East End because that is the only place where people do not wear masks upon their faces, but I have told her that I live in the West End because nothing in life interests me but the mask.'

We read our poems to one another and talked criticism and drank a little wine. I sometimes say when I speak of the club, 'We had such and such ideas, such and such a quarrel with the great Victorians, we set before us such and such aims,' as though we had many philosophical ideas. I say this because I am ashamed to admit that I had these ideas and that whenever I began to talk of them a gloomy silence fell upon the room. A young Irish poet, who wrote excellently but had the worst manners, was to say a few years later, 'You do not talk like a poet, you talk like a man of letters;' and if all the rhymers had not been polite, if most of them had not been to Oxford or Cambridge, they would have said the same thing. I was full of thought, often very abstract thought, longing all the while to be full of images, because I had gone to the art school instead of a university. Yet even if I had gone to a university, and learned all the classical foundations of English literature and English culture, all that great erudition which, once accepted, frees the mind from restlessness, I should have had to give up my Irish subject matter, or attempt to found a new tradition. Lacking sufficient recognised precedent I must needs find out some reason for all I did. I knew almost from the start that to overflow with reasons was to be not quite well-born, and when I could I hid them, as men hide a disagreeable ancestry; and that there was no help for it, seeing that my country was not born at all. I was of those doomed to imperfect achievement, and under a curse, as it were, like some race of birds compelled to spend the time, needed for the making of the nest, in argument as to the convenience of moss and twig and lichen. Le Gallienne and Davidson, and even Symons, were provincial at their setting out, but their provincialism was curable, mine incurable; while the one conviction shared by all the younger men, but principally by Johnson and Horne, who imposed their personalities upon us, was an opposition to all ideas, all generalisations that can be explained and debated. E... fresh from Paris would sometimes say, 'We are concerned with nothing but impressions,' but that itself was a generalisation and met but stony silence. Conversation constantly dwindled into 'Do you like so and so's last book?' 'No, I prefer the book before it,' and I think that but for its Irish members, who said whatever came into their heads, the club would not have survived its first difficult months. I knew, now ashamed that I thought 'like a man of letters,' now exasperated at their indifference to the fashion of their own river bed, that Swinburne in one way, Browning in another, and Tennyson in a third, had filled their work with what I called 'impurities,' curiosities about politics, about science, about history, about religion; and that we must create once more the pure work.

Our clothes were for the most part unadventurous like our conversation, though I indeed wore a brown velveteen coat, a loose tie and a very old Inverness cape, discarded by my father twenty years before and preserved by my Sligo-born mother whose actions were unreasoning and habitual like the seasons. But no other member of the club, except Le Gallienne, who wore a loose tie, and Symons, who had an Inverness cape that was quite new & almost fashionable, would have shown himself for the world in any costume but 'that of an English gentleman.' 'One should be quite unnoticeable,' Johnson explained to me. Those who conformed most carefully to the fashion in their clothes generally departed furthest from it in their hand-writing, which was small, neat and studied, one poet, which I forget, having founded his upon the handwriting of George Herbert. Dowson and Symons I was to know better in later years when Symons became a very dear friend, and I never got behind John Davidson's Scottish roughness and exasperation, though I saw much of him, but from the first I devoted myself to Lionel Johnson. He and Horne and Image and one or two others shared a man-servant and an old house in Charlotte Street, Fitzroy Square, typical figures of transition, doing as an achievement of learning and of exquisite taste what their predecessors did in careless abundance. All were Pre-Raphaelite, and sometimes one might meet in the rooms of one or other a ragged figure, as of some fallen dynasty, Simeon Solomon, the Pre- Raphaelite painter, once the friend of Rossetti and of Swinburne, but fresh now from some low public house. Condemned to a long term of imprisonment for a criminal offence, he had sunk into drunkenness and misery. Introduced one night, however, to some man who mistook him, in the dim candle light, for another Solomon, a successful academic painter and R. A., he started to his feet in a rage with 'Sir, do you dare to mistake me for that mountebank?' Though not one had harkened to the feeblest caw, or been spattered by the smallest dropping from any Huxley, Tyndall, Carolus Duran, Bastien-Lepage bundle of old twigs, I began by suspecting them of lukewarmness, and even backsliding, and I owe it to that suspicion that I never became intimate with Horne, who lived to become the greatest English authority upon Italian life in the fourteenth century and to write the one standard work on Botticelli. Connoisseur in several arts, he had designed a little church in the manner of Inigo Jones for a burial ground near the Marble Arch. Though I now think his little church a masterpiece, its style was more than a century too late to hit my fancy at two or three and twenty; and I accused him of leaning towards that eighteenth century

That taught a school
Of dolts to smooth, inlay, and clip, and fit
Till, like the certain wands of Jacob's wit,
Their verses tallied.

Another fanaticism delayed my friendship with two men, who are now my friends and in certain matters my chief instructors. Somebody, probably Lionel Johnson, brought me to the studio of Charles Ricketts and Charles Shannon, certainly heirs of the great generation, and the first thing I saw was a Shannon picture of a lady and child arrayed in lace, silk and satin, suggesting that hated century. My eyes were full of some more mythological mother and child and I would have none of it, and I told Shannon that he had not painted a mother and child but elegant people expecting visitors and I thought that a great reproach. Somebody writing in 'The Germ' had said that a picture of a pheasant and an apple was merely a picture of something to eat, and I was so angry with the indifference to subject, which was the commonplace of all art criticism since Bastien-Lepage, that I could at times see nothing else but subject. I thought that, though it might not matter to the man himself whether he loved a white woman or a black, a female pickpocket or a regular communicant of the Church of England, if only he loved strongly, it certainly did matter to his relations and even under some circumstances to his whole neighbourhood. Sometimes indeed, like some father in Moliere, I ignored the lover's feelings altogether and even refused to admit that a trace of the devil, perhaps a trace of colour, may lend piquancy, especially if the connection be not permanent.

Among these men, of whom so many of the greatest talents were to live such passionate lives and die such tragic deaths, one serene man, T. W. Rolleston, seemed always out of place. It was I brought him there, intending to set him to some work in Ireland later on. I have known young Dublin working men slip out of their workshop to see 'the second Thomas Davis' passing by, and even remember a conspiracy, by some three or four, to make him 'the leader of the Irish race at home & abroad,' and all because he had regular features; and when all is said, Alexander the Great & Alcibiades were personable men, and the Founder of the Christian religion was the only man who was neither a little too tall nor a little too short but exactly six feet high. We in Ireland thought as do the plays and ballads, not understanding that, from the first moment wherein nature foresaw the birth of Bastien-Lepage, she has only granted great creative power to men whose faces are contorted with extravagance or curiosity or dulled with some protecting stupidity.

I had now met all those who were to make the nineties of the last century tragic in the history of literature, but as yet we were all seemingly equal, whether in talent or in luck, and scarce even personalities to one another. I remember saying one night at the Cheshire Cheese, when more poets than usual had come, 'None of us can say who will succeed, or even who has or has not talent. The only thing certain about us is that we are too many.'

XVII

I have described what image, always opposite to the natural self or the natural world, Wilde, Henley, Morris copied or tried to copy, but I have not said if I found an image for myself. I know very little about myself and much less of that anti-self: probably the woman who cooks my dinner or the woman who sweeps out my study knows more than I. It is perhaps because nature made me a gregarious man, going hither and thither looking for conversation, and ready to deny from fear or favour his dearest conviction, that I love proud and lonely images. When I was a child and went daily to the sexton's daughter for writing lessons, I found one poem in her School Reader that delighted me beyond all others: a fragment of some metrical translation from Aristophanes wherein the birds sing scorn upon mankind. In later years my mind gave itself to gregarious Shelley's dream of a young man, his hair blanched with sorrow studying philosophy in some lonely tower, or of his old man, master of all human knowledge, hidden from human sight in some shell-strewn cavern on the Mediterranean shore. One passage above all ran perpetually in my ears

Some feign that he is Enoch: others dream
He was pre-Adamite, and has survived
Cycles of generation and of ruin.
The sage, in truth, by dreadful abstinence,
And conquering penance of the mutinous flesh,
Deep contemplation and unwearied study,

In years outstretched beyond the date of man,
May have attained to sovereignty and science
Over those strong and secret things and thoughts
Which others fear and know not.

MAHMUD
I would talk
With this old Jew.

HASSAN
Thy will is even now
Made known to him where he dwells in a sea-cavern
'Mid the Demonesi, less accessible
Than thou or God! He who would question him
Must sail alone at sunset where the stream
Of ocean sleeps around those foamless isles,
When the young moon is westering as now,
And evening airs wander upon the wave;
And, when the pines of that bee-pasturing isle,
Green Erebinthus, quench the fiery shadow
Of his gilt prow within the sapphire water,
Then must the lonely helmsman cry aloud
'Ahasuerus!' and the caverns round
Will answer 'Ahasuerus!' If his prayer
Be granted, a faint meteor will arise,
Lighting him over Marmora; and a wind
Will rush out of the sighing pine-forest,
And with the wind a storm of harmony
Unutterably sweet, and pilot him
Through the soft twilight to the Bosphorus:
Thence, at the hour and place and circumstance
Fit for the matter of their conference,
The Jew appears. Few dare, and few who dare
Win the desired communion.

Already in Dublin, I had been attracted to the Theosophists because they had affirmed the real existence of the Jew, or of his like; and, apart from whatever might have been imagined by Huxley, Tyndall, Carolus Duran and Bastien-Lepage, I saw nothing against his reality. Presently having heard that Madame Blavatsky had arrived from France, or from India, I thought it time to look the matter up. Certainly if wisdom existed anywhere in the world it must be in some such lonely mind admitting no duty to us, communing with God only, conceding nothing from fear or favour. Have not all peoples, while bound together in a single mind and taste, believed that such men existed and paid them that honour, or paid it to their mere shadow, which they have refused to philanthropists and to men of learning?

I found Madame Blavatsky in a little house at Norwood, with but, as she said, three followers left, the Society of Psychical Research had just reported on her Indian phenomena, and as one of the three followers sat in an outer room to keep out undesirable visitors, I was kept a long time kicking my heels. Presently I was admitted and found an old woman in a plain loose dark dress: a sort of old Irish peasant woman with an air of humour and audacious power. I was still kept waiting, for she was deep in conversation with a woman visitor. I strayed through folding doors into the next room and stood, in sheer idleness of mind, looking at a cuckoo clock. It was certainly stopped, for the weights were off and lying upon the ground, and yet as I stood there the cuckoo came out and cuckooed at me. I interrupted Madame Blavatsky to say. 'Your clock has hooted me.' 'It often hoots at a stranger,' she replied. 'Is there a spirit in it?' I said. 'I do not know,' she said, 'I should have to be alone to know what is in it.' I went back to the clock and began examining it and heard her say 'Do not break my clock.' I wondered if there was some hidden mechanism, and I should have been put out, I suppose, had I found any, though Henley had said to me, 'Of course she gets up fraudulent miracles, but a person of genius has to do something; Sarah Bernhardt sleeps in her coffin.' Presently the visitor went away and Madame Blavatsky explained that she was a propagandist for women's rights who had called to find out 'why men were so bad.' 'What explanation did you give her?' I said. 'That men were born bad but women made themselves so,' and then she explained that I had been kept waiting because she had mistaken me for some man whose name resembled mine and who wanted to persuade her of the flatness of the earth.

When I next saw her she had moved into a house at Holland Park, and some time must have passed, probably I had been in Sligo where I returned constantly for long visits, for she was surrounded by followers. She sat nightly before a little table covered with green baize and on this green baize she scribbled constantly with a piece of white chalk. She would scribble symbols, sometimes humorously applied, and sometimes unintelligible figures, but the chalk was intended to mark down her score when she played patience. One saw in the next room a large table where every night her followers and guests, often a great number, sat down to their vegetarian meal, while she encouraged or mocked through the folding doors. A great passionate nature, a sort of female Dr. Johnson, impressive, I think, to every man or woman who had themselves any richness, she seemed impatient of the formalism, of the shrill abstract idealism of those about her, and this impatience broke out inrailing & many nicknames: 'O you are a flapdoodle, but then you are a theosophist and a brother. 'The most devout and learned of all her followers said to me, 'H.P.B. has just told me that there is another globe stuck on to this at the north pole, so that the earth has really a shape something like a dumb-bell.' I said, for I knew that her imagination contained all the folklore of the world, 'That must be some piece of Eastern mythology.' 'O no it is not,' he said, 'of that I am certain, and there must be something in it or she would not have said it.' Her mockery was not kept for her followers alone, and her voice would become harsh, and her mockery lose phantasy and humour, when she spoke of what seemed to her scientific materialism. Once I saw this antagonism, guided by some kind of telepathic divination, take a form of brutal phantasy. I brought a very able Dublin woman to see her and this woman had a brother, a physiologist whose reputation, though known to specialists alone, was European; and, because of this brother, a family pride in everything scientific and modern. The Dublin woman scarcely opened her mouth the whole evening and her name was certainly unknown to Madame Blavatsky, yet I saw at once in that wrinkled old face bent over the cards, and the only time I ever saw it there, a personal hostility, the dislike of one woman for another. Madame Blavatsky seemed to bundle herself up, becoming all primeval peasant, and began complaining of her ailments, more especially of her bad leg. But of late her master, her 'old Jew,' her 'Ahasuerus,' cured it, or set it on the way to be cured. 'I was sitting here in my chair,' she said, 'when the master came in and brought something with him which he put over my knee, something warm which enclosed my knee, it was a live dog which he had cut open.' I recognised a cure used sometimes in mediaeval medicine. She had two masters, and their portraits, ideal Indian heads, painted by some most incompetent artist, stood upon either side of the folding doors. One night, when talk was impersonal and general, I sat gazing through the folding doors into the dimly lighted dining-room beyond. I noticed a curious red light shining upon a picture and got up to see where the red light came from. It was the picture of an Indian and as I came near it slowly vanished. When I returned to my seat, Madame Blavatsky said, 'What did you see?' 'A picture,' I said. 'Tell it to go away.' 'It is already gone.' 'So much the better,' she said, 'I was afraid it was medium ship but it is only clairvoyance.' 'What is the difference?' 'If it had been medium ship, it would have stayed in spite of you. Beware of medium ship; it is a kind of madness; I know, for I have been through it.'

I found her almost always full of gaiety that, unlike the occasional joking of those about her, was illogical and incalculable and yet always kindly and tolerant. I had called one evening to find her absent, but expected every moment. She had been somewhere at the seaside for her health and arrived with a little suite of followers. She sat down at once in her big chair, and began unfolding a brown paper parcel, while all looked on full of curiosity. It contained a large family Bible. 'This is a present for my maid,' she said. 'What! A Bible and not even anointed!' said some shocked voice. 'Well my children,' was the answer, 'what is the good of giving lemons to those who want oranges?' When I first began to frequent her house, as I soon did very constantly, I noticed a handsome clever woman of the world there, who seemed certainly very much out of place, penitent though she thought herself. Presently there was much scandal and gossip, for the penitent was plainly entangled with two young men, who were expected to grow into ascetic sages. The scandal was so great that Madame Blavatsky had to call the penitent before her and to speak after this fashion, 'We think that it is necessary to crush the animal nature; you should live in chastity in act and thought. Initiation is granted only to those who are entirely chaste,' and so to run on for some time. However, after some minutes in that vehement style, the penitent standing crushed and shamed before her, she had wound up, 'I cannot permit you more than one.' She was quite sincere, but thought that nothing mattered but what happened in the mind, and that if we could not master the mind, our actions were of little importance. One young man filled her with exasperation; for she thought that his settled gloom came from his chastity. I had known him in Dublin, where he had been accustomed to interrupt long periods of asceticism, in which he would eat vegetables and drink water, with brief outbreaks of what he considered the devil. After an outbreak he would for a few hours dazzle the imagination of the members of the local theosophical society with poetical rhapsodies about harlots and street lamps, and then sink into weeks of melancholy. A fellow theosophist once found him hanging from the window pole, but cut him down in the nick of time. I said to the man who cut him down, 'What did you say to one another?' He said, 'We spent the night telling comic stories and laughing a great deal.' This man, torn between sensuality and visionary ambition, was now the most devout of all, and told me that in the middle of the night he could often hear the ringing of the little 'astral bell' whereby Madame Blavatsky's master called her attention, and that, although it was a low silvery sound it made the whole house shake. Another night I found him waiting in the hall to show in those who had the right of entrance on some night when the discussion was private, and as I passed he whispered into my ear, 'Madame Blavatsky is perhaps not a real woman at all. They say that her dead body was found many years ago upon some Russian battlefield.' She had two dominant moods, both of extreme activity, but one calm and philosophic, and this was the mood always on that night in the week, when she answered questions upon her system; and as I look back after thirty years I often ask myself 'Was her speech automatic? Was she for one night, in every week, a trance medium, or in some similar state?' In the other mood she was full of phantasy and inconsequent raillery. 'That is the Greek church, a triangle like all true religion,' I recall her saying, as she chalked out a triangle on the green baize, and then, as she made it disappear in meaningless scribbles 'it spread out and became a bramble-bush like the Church of Rome.' Then rubbing it all out except one straight line, 'Now they have lopped off the branches and turned it into a broomstick arid that is Protestantism.' And so it was, night after night, always varied and unforseen. I have observed a like sudden extreme change in others, half whose thought was supernatural, and Laurence Oliphant records somewhere or other like observations. I can remember only once finding her in a mood of reverie; something had happened to damp her spirits, some attack upon her movement, or upon herself. She spoke of Balzac, whom she had seen but once, of Alfred de Musset, whom she had known well enough to dislike for his morbidity, and of George Sand whom she had known so well that they had dabbled in magic together of which 'neither knew anything at all' in those days; and she ran on, as if there was nobody there to overhear her, 'I used to wonder at and pity the people who sell their souls to the devil, but now I only pity them. They do it to have somebody on their sides,' and added to that, after some words I have forgotten, 'I write, write, write as the Wandering Jew walks, walks, walks.' Besides the devotees, who came to listen and to turn every doctrine into a new sanction for the puritanical convictions of their Victorian childhood, cranks came from half Europe and from all America, and they came that they might talk. One American said to me, 'She has become the most famous woman in the world by sitting in a big chair and permitting us to talk.' They talked and she played patience, and totted up her score on the green baize, and generally seemed to listen, but sometimes she would listen no more. There was a woman who talked perpetually of 'the divine spark' within her, until Madame Blavatsky stopped her with, 'Yes, my dear, you have a divine spark within you, and if you are not very careful you will hear it snore.' A certain Salvation Army captain probably pleased her, for, if vociferous and loud of voice, he had much animation. He had known hardship and spoke of his visions while starving in the streets and he was still perhaps a little light in the head. I wondered what he could preach to ignorant men, his head ablaze with wild mysticism, till I met a man who had heard him talking near Covent Garden to some crowd in the street. 'My friends,' he was saying, 'you have the kingdom of heaven within you and it would take a pretty big pill to get that out.'

XVIII

Meanwhile I had not got any nearer to proving that 'Ahasuerus dwells in a sea-cavern 'mid the Demonesi,' but one conclusion I certainly did come to, which I find written out in an old diary and dated 1887. Madame Blavatsky's 'masters' were 'trance' personalities, but by 'trance personalities' I meant something almost as exciting as 'Ahasuerus' himself. Years before I had found, on a table in the Royal Irish Academy, a pamphlet on Japanese art, and read there of an animal painter so remarkable that horses he had painted upon a temple wall had stepped down after and trampled the neighbouring fields of rice. Somebody had come to the temple in the early morning, been startled by a shower of water drops, looked up and seen a painted horse, still wet from the dew-covered fields, but now 'trembling into stillness.' I thought that her masters were imaginary forms created by suggestion, but whether that suggestion came from Madame Blavatsky's own mind or from some mind, perhaps at a great distance, I did not know; and I believed that these forms could pass from Madame Blavatsky's mind to the minds of others, and even acquire external reality, and that it was even possible that they talked and wrote. They were born in the imagination, where Blake had declared that all men live after death, and where 'every man is king or priest in his own house.' Certainly the house at Holland Park was a romantic place, where one heard of constant apparitions and exchanged speculations like those of the middle ages, and I did not separate myself from it by my own will. The Secretary, an intelligent and friendly man, asked me to come and see him, and when I did, complained that I was causing discussion and disturbance, a certain fanatical hungry face had been noticed red and tearful, & it was quite plain that I was not in full agreement with their method or their philosophy. 'I know,' he said, 'that all these people become dogmatic and fanatical because they believe what they can never prove; that their withdrawal from family life is to them a great misfortune; but what are we to do? We have been told that all spiritual influx into the society will come to an end in 1897 for exactly one hundred years. Before that date our fundamental ideas must be spread through the world.' I knew the doctrine and it had made me wonder why that old woman, or rather 'the trance personalities' who directed her and were her genius, insisted upon it, for influx of some kind there must always be. Did they dread heresy after the death of Madame Blavatsky, or had they no purpose but the greatest possible immediate effort?

XIX

At the British Museum reading-room I often saw a man of thirty-six or thirty-seven, in a brown velveteen coat, with a gaunt resolute face, and an athletic body, who seemed before I heard his name, or knew the nature of his studies, a figure of romance. Presently I was introduced, where or by what man or woman I do not remember. He was Macgregor Mathers, the author of the 'Kabbalas Unveiled,' & his studies were two only, magic and the theory of war, for he believed himself a born commander and all but equal in wisdom and in power to that old Jew. He had copied many manuscripts on magic ceremonial and doctrine in the British Museum, and was to copy many more in continental libraries, and it was through him mainly that I began certain studies and experiences that were to convince me that images well up before the mind's eye from a deeper source than conscious or subconscious memory. I believe that his mind in those early days did not belie his face and body, though in later years it became unhinged, for he kept a proud head amid great poverty. One that boxed with him nightly has told me that for many weeks he could knock him down, though Macgregor was the stronger man, and only knew long after that during those weeks Macgregor starved. With him I met an old white-haired Oxfordshire clergyman, the most panic-stricken person I have ever known, though Macgregor's introduction had been 'He unites us to the great adepts of antiquity.' This old man took me aside that he might say, 'I hope you never invoke spirits, that is a very dangerous thing to do. I am told that even the planetary spirits turn upon us in the end.' I said, 'Have you ever seen an apparition?' 'O yes, once,' he said. 'I have my alchemical laboratory in a cellar under my house where the Bishop cannot see it. One day I was walking up & down there when I heard another footstep walking up and down beside me. I turned and saw a girl I had been in love with when I was a young man, but she died long ago. She wanted me to kiss her. Oh no, I would not do that.' 'Why not?' I said. 'Oh, she might have got power over me.' 'Has your alchemical research had any success?' I said. 'Yes, I once made the elixir of life. A French alchemist said it had the right smell and the right colour,' (The alchemist may have been Elephas Levi, who visited England in the sixties, & would have said anything) 'but the first effect of the elixir is that your nails fall out and your hair falls off. I was afraid that I might have made a mistake and that nothing else might happen, so I put it away on a shelf. I meant to drink it when I was an old man, but when I got it down the other day it had all dried up.'

XX

I generalized a great deal and was ashamed of it. I thought that it was my business in life to be an artist and a poet, and that there could be no business comparable to that. I refused to read books, and even to meet people who excited me to generalization, but all to no purpose. I said my prayers much as in childhood, though without the old regularity of hour and place, and I began to pray that my imagination might somehow be rescued from abstraction, and become as pre-occupied with life as had been the imagination of Chaucer. For ten or twelve years more I suffered continual remorse, and only became content when my abstractions had composed themselves into picture and dramatization. My very remorse helped to spoil my early poetry, giving it an element of sentimentality through my refusal to permit it any share of an intellect which I considered impure. Even in practical life I only very gradually began to use generalizations, that have since become the foundation of all I have done, or shall do, in Ireland. For all I know, all men may have been as timid; for I am persuaded that our intellects at twenty contain all the truths we shall ever find, but as yet we do not know truths that belong to us from opinions caught up in casual irritation or momentary phantasy. As life goes on we discover that certain thoughts sustain us in defeat, or give us victory, whether over ourselves or others, & it is these thoughts, tested by passion, that we call convictions. Among subjective men (in all those, that is, who must spin a web out of their own bowels) the victory is an intellectual daily recreation of all that exterior fate snatches away, and so that fate's antithesis; while what I have called 'The mask' is an emotional antithesis to all that comes out of their internal nature. We begin to live when we have conceived life as a tragedy.

A conviction that the world was now but a bundle of fragments possessed me without ceasing. I had tried this conviction on 'The Rhymers,' thereby plunging into greater silence an already too silent evening. 'Johnson,' I was accustomed to say, 'you are the only man I know whose silence has beak & claw.' I had lectured on it to some London Irish society, and I was to lecture upon it later on in Dublin, but I never found but one interested man, an official of the Primrose League, who was also an active member of the Fenian Brotherhood. 'I am an extreme conservative apart from Ireland,' I have heard him explain; and I have no doubt that personal experience made him share the sight of any eye that saw the world in fragments. I had been put into a rage by the followers of Huxley, Tyndall, Carolus Duran and Bastien-Lepage, who not only asserted the unimportance of subject, whether in art or literature, but the independence of the arts from one another. Upon the other hand I delighted in every age where poet and artist confined themselves gladly to some inherited subject matter known to the whole people, for I thought that in man and race alike there is something called 'unity of being,' using that term as Dante used it when he compared beauty in the Convito to a perfectly proportioned human body. My father, from whom I had learned the term, preferred a comparison to a musical instrument so strong that if we touch a string all the strings murmur faintly. There is not more desire, he had said, in lust than in true love; but in true love desire awakens pity, hope, affection, admiration, and, given appropriate circumstance, every emotion possible to man. When I began, however, to apply this thought to the State and to argue for a law-made balance among trades and occupations, my father displayed at once the violent free-trader and propagandist of liberty. I thought that the enemy of this unity was abstraction, meaning by abstraction not the distinction but the isolation of occupation, or class or faculty

'Call down the hawk from the air
Let him be hooded, or caged,
Till the yellow eye has grown mild,
For larder and spit are bare,
The old cook enraged,
The scullion gone wild.'

I knew no mediaeval cathedral, and Westminster, being a part of abhorred London, did not interest me; but I thought constantly of Homer and Dante and the tombs of Mausolus and Artemisa, the great figures of King and Queen and the lesser figures of Greek and Amazon, Centaur and Greek. I thought that all art should be a Centaur finding in the popular lore its back and its strong legs. I got great pleasure too from remembering that Homer was sung, and from that tale of Dante hearing a common man sing some stanza from 'The Divine Comedy,' and from Don Quixote's meeting with some common man that sang Ariosto. Morris had never seemed to care for any poet later than Chaucer; and though I preferred Shakespeare to Chaucer I begrudged my own preference. Had not Europe shared one mind and heart, until both mind and heart began to break into fragments a little before Shakespeare's birth? Music and verse began to fall apart when Chaucer robbed verse of its speed that he might give it greater meditation, though for another generation or so minstrels were to sing his long elaborated 'Troilus and Cressida;' painting parted from religion in the later Renaissance that it might study effects of tangibility undisturbed; while, that it might characterise, where it had once personified, it renounced, in our own age, all that inherited subject matter which we have named poetry. Presently I was indeed to number character itself among the abstractions, encouraged by Congreve's saying that 'passions are too powerful in the fair sex to let humour,' or as we say character, 'have its course.' Nor have we fared better under the common daylight, for pure reason has notoriously made but light of practical reason, and has been made but light of in its turn, from that morning when Descartes discovered that he could think better in his bed than out of it; nor needed I original thought to discover, being so late of the school of Morris, that machinery had not separated from handicraft wholly for the world's good; nor to notice that the distinction of classes had become their isolation. If the London merchants of our day competed together in writing lyrics they would not, like the Tudor merchants, dance in the open street before the house of the victor; nor do the great ladies of London finish their balls on the pavement before their doors as did the great Venetian ladies even in the eighteenth century, conscious of an all enfolding sympathy. Doubtless because fragments broke into even smaller fragments we saw one another in a light of bitter comedy, and in the arts, where now one technical element reigned and now another, generation hated generation, and accomplished beauty was snatched away when it had most engaged our affections. One thing I did not foresee, not having the courage of my own thought, the growing murderousness of the world.

Turning and turning in the widening gyre
The falcon cannot hear the falconer;
Things fall apart; the centre cannot hold;
Mere anarchy is loosed upon the world,
The blood-dimmed tide is loosed, and everywhere
The ceremony of innocence is drowned;
The best lack all conviction, while the worst
Are full of passionate intensity.

XXII

The Huxley, Tyndall, Carolus Duran, Bastien-Lepage coven asserted that an artist or a poet must paint or write in the style of his own day, and this with 'The Fairy Queen,' and 'Lyrical Ballads,' and Blake's early poems in its ears, and plain to the eyes, in book or gallery, those great masterpieces of later Egypt, founded upon that work of the Ancient Kingdom already further in time from later Egypt than later Egypt is from us. I knew that I could choose my style where I pleased, that no man can deny to the human mind any power, that power once achieved; and yet I did not wish to recover the first simplicity. If I must be but a shepherd building his hut among the ruins of some fallen city, I might take porphyry or shaped marble, if it lay ready to my hand, instead of the baked clay of the first builders. If Chaucer's personages had disengaged themselves from Chaucer's crowd, forgotten their common goal and shrine, and after sundry magnifications become, each in his turn, the centre of some Elizabethan play, and a few years later split into their elements, and so given birth to romantic poetry, I need not reverse the cinematograph. I could take those separated elements, all that abstract love and melancholy, and give them a symbolical or mythological coherence. Not Chaucer's rough-tongued riders, but some procession of the Gods! a pilgrimage no more but perhaps a shrine! Might I not, with health and good luck to aid me, create some new 'Prometheus Unbound,' Patrick or Columbcille, Oisin or Fion, in Prometheus's stead, and, instead of Caucasus, Croagh-Patrick or Ben Bulben? Have not all races had their first unity from a polytheism that marries them to rock and hill? We had in Ireland imaginative stories, which the uneducated classes knew and even sang, and might we not make those stories current among the educated classes, re-discovering for the work's sake what I have called 'the applied arts of literature,' the association of literature, that is, with music, speech and dance; and at last, it might be, so deepen the political passion of the nation that all, artist and poet, craftsman and day labourer would accept a common design? Perhaps even these images, once created and associated with river and mountain, might move of themselves, and with some powerful even turbulent life, like those painted horses that trampled the rice fields of Japan.

XXIII

I used to tell the few friends to whom I could speak these secret thoughts that I would make the attempt in Ireland but fail, for our civilisation, its elements multiplying by divisions like certain low forms of life, was all powerful; but in reality I had the wildest hopes. To-day I add to that first conviction, to that first desire for unity, this other conviction, long a mere opinion vaguely or intermittently apprehended: Nations, races and individual men are unified by an image, or bundle of related images, symbolical or evocative of the state of mind, which is of all states of mind not impossible, the most difficult to that man, race or nation; because only the greatest obstacle that can be contemplated without despair rouses the will to full intensity. A powerful class by terror, rhetoric, and organised sentimentality, may drive their people to war, but the day draws near when they cannot keep them there; and how shall they face the pure nations of the East when the day comes to do it with but equal arms? I had seen Ireland in my own time turn from the bragging rhetoric and gregarious humour of O'Connell's generation and school, and offer herself to the solitary and proud Parnell as to her anti-self, buskin following hard on sock; and I had begun to hope, or to half-hope, that we might be the first in Europe to seek unity as deliberately as it had been sought by theologian, poet, sculptor, architect from the eleventh to the thirteenth century. Doubtless we must seek it differently, no longer considering it convenient to epitomise all human knowledge, but find it we well might, could we first find philosophy and a little passion.

XXIV

It was the death of Parnell that convinced me that the moment had come for work in Ireland, for I knew that for a time the imagination of young men would turn from politics. There was a little Irish patriotic society of young people, clerks, shop-boys, shop-girls, and the like, called the Southwark Irish Literary Society. It had ceased to meet because each member of the committee had lectured so many times that the girls got the giggles whenever he stood up. I invited the committee to my father's house at Bedford Park and there proposed a new organisation. After a few months spent in founding, with the help of T. W. Rolleston, who came to that first meeting and had a knowledge of committee work I lacked, the Irish Literary Society, which soon included every London Irish author and journalist, I went to Dublin and founded there a similar society.

BOOK II

IRELAND AFTER THE FALL OF PARNELL

I

A couple of years before the death of Parnell, I had wound up my introduction to those selections from the Irish novelists with the prophecy of an intellectual movement at the first lull in politics, and now I wished to fulfil my prophecy. I did not put it in that way, for I preferred to think that the sudden emotion that now came to me, the sudden certainty that Ireland was to be like soft wax for years to come, was a moment of supernatural insight. How could I tell, how can I tell even now?

There was a little Irish Society of young people, clerks, shop boys, and shop girls, called "The Southwark Irish Literary Society," and it had ceased to meet because the girls got the giggles when any member of the Committee got up to speak. Every member of it had said all he had to say many times over. I had given them a lecture about the falling asunder of the human mind, as an opening flower falls asunder, and all had professed admiration because I had made such a long speech without quotation or narrative; and now I invited the Committee to my father's house at Bedford Park, and there proposed a new organization, "The Irish Literary Society." T. W. Rolleston came to that first meeting, and it was because he had much tact, and a knowledge of the technical business of committees, that a society was founded which was joined by every London-Irish author and journalist. In a few months somebody had written its history, and published that history, illustrated by our portraits, at a shilling. When it was published I was in Dublin, founding a society there called "The National Literary Society," and affiliating it with certain Young Ireland Societies in country towns which seemed anxious to accept its leadership. I had definite plans; I wanted to create an Irish Theatre; I was finishing my Countess Cathleen in its first meagre version, and thought of a travelling company to visit our country branches; but before that there must be a popular imaginative literature. I arranged with Mr. Fisher Unwin and his reader, Mr Edward Garnett, a personal friend of mine, that when our organization was complete Mr Fisher Unwin was to publish for it a series of books at a shilling each. I told only one man of this arrangement, for after I had made my plans I heard an alarming rumour. Old Sir Charles Gavan Duffy was coming from Australia to start an Irish publishing house, and publish a series of books, and I did not expect to agree with him, but knew that I must not seek a quarrel. The two societies were necessary because their lectures must take the place of an educated popular press, which we had not, and have not now, and create a standard of criticism. Irish literature had fallen into contempt; no educated man ever bought an Irish book; in Dublin Professor Dowden, the one man of letters with an international influence, was accustomed to say that he knew an Irish book by its smell, because he had once seen some books whose binding had been fastened together by rotten glue; and Standish O'Grady's last book upon ancient Irish history, a book rather wild, rather too speculative, but forestalling later research, had not been reviewed by any periodical or newspaper in England or in Ireland.

At first I had great success, for I brought with me a list of names written down by some member of the Southwark Irish Literary Society, and for six weeks went hither and thither appealing and persuading. My first conversation was over a butter-tub in some Dublin back street, and the man agreed with me at once; everybody agreed with me; all felt that something must be done, but nobody knew what. Perhaps they did not understand me, perhaps I kept back my full thoughts, perhaps they only seemed to listen; it was enough that I had a plan, and was determined about it. When I went to lecture in a provincial town, a workman's wife, who wrote patriotic stories in some weekly newspaper, invited me to her house, and I found all her children in their Sunday best. She made a little speech, very formal and very simple, in which she said that what she wrote had no merit, but that it paid for her children's schooling; and she finished her speech by telling her children never to forget that they had seen me. One man compared me to Thomas Davis, another said I could organise like Davitt, and I thought to succeed as they did, and as rapidly. I did not examine this applause, nor the true thoughts of those I met, nor the general condition of the country, but I examined myself a great deal, and was puzzled at myself. I knew that I was shy and timid, that I would often leave some business undone, or purchase unmade, because I shrank from facing a strange office or a shop a little grander than usual, and yet, here was I delightedly talking to strange people every day. It was many years before I understood that I had surrendered myself to the chief temptation of the artist, creation without toil. Metrical composition is always very difficult to me, nothing is done upon the first day, not one rhyme is in its place; and when at last the rhymes begin to come, the first rough draft of a six-line stanza takes the whole day. At that time I had not formed a style, and sometimes a six-line stanza would take several days, and not seem finished even then; and I had not learnt, as I have now, to put it all out of my head before night, and so the last night was generally sleepless, and the last day a day of nervous strain. But now I had found the happiness that Shelley found when he tied a pamphlet to a fire balloon.

II

At first I asked no help from prominent persons, and when some clerk or shop-assistant would say "Dr So-and-so or Professor So-and-so will have nothing to do with us" I would answer, "When we prove we can gather sheep shepherds will come." Presently, come they did, old, middle-aged, or but little older than myself, but all with some authority in their town: John O'Leary, John F. Taylor, and Douglas Hyde, and Standish O'Grady, and of these much presently; Dr. Sigerson who has picked a quarrel with me and of whom I shall say nothing that he may not pick another; Count Plunkett, Sinn Feiner of late and Minister of Dail Eireann; Dr. Coffey, now head of the National University; George Coffey, later on Curator of the Irish Antiquities at the Museum of the Royal Dublin Society; Patrick J. McCall, poet and publican of Patrick Street, and later member of corporation; Richard Ashe King, novelist and correspondent of Truth, a gentle, intelligent person, typical of nothing; and others, known or unknown. We were now important, had our Committee room in the Mansion House, and I remember that the old Mansion House butler recognised our importance so fully, that he took us into his confidence once in every week, while we sat waiting for a quorum. He had seen many Lord Mayors, and remembered those very superior Lord Mayors who lived before the extension of the municipal franchise, and spoke of his present masters with contempt. Among our persons of authority, and among the friends and followers they had brought, there were many who at that time found it hard to refuse if anybody offered for sale a pepper-pot shaped to suggest a round tower with a wolf-dog at its foot, and who would have felt it inappropriate to publish an Irish book, that had not harp and shamrock and green cover, so completely did their minds move amid Young Ireland images and metaphors, and I thought with alarm of the coming of Sir Charles Gavan Duffy; while here and there I noticed that smooth, smiling face that we discover for the first time in certain pictures by Velasquez; all that hungry, mediaeval speculation vanished, that had worn the faces of El Greco and in its place a self-complacent certainty that all had been arranged, provided for, set out in clear type, in manual of devotion or of doctrine. These, however, were no true disciples of Young Ireland, for Young Ireland had sought a nation unified by political doctrine, a subservient art and letters aiding and abetting. The movement of thought, which had in the 'fifties and 'fourties at Paris and London and Boston, filled literature, and especially poetical literature with curiosities about science, about history about politics, with moral purpose and educational fervour, abstractions all, had created a new instrument for Irish politics, a method of writing that took its poetical style from Campbell, Scott, Macauley, and Beranger, with certain elements from Gaelic, and its prose style, in John Mitchell, the only Young Ireland prose writer who had a style at all, from Carlyle. To recommend this method of writing as literature without much reservation and discrimination I contended was to be deceived or to practice deception. If one examined some country love-song, one discovered that it was not written by a man in love, but by a patriot who wanted to prove that we did indeed possess, in the words of Daniel O'Connell, "the finest peasantry upon earth." Yet one well-known anthology was introduced by the assertion that such love-poetry was superior to "affected and artificial" English love-songs like "Drink to me only with thine eyes", "affected and artificial," the very words used by English Victorians who wrote for the newspapers to discourage capricious, personal writing. However, the greater number even of those who thought our famous anthology, The Spirit of the Nation, except for three or four songs, but good election rhyme, looked upon it much as certain enlightened believers look upon the story of Adam and Eve and the apple, or that of Jonah and the whale, which they do not question publicly, because such stories are an integral part of religion to simple men and women. I, upon the other hand, being in the intemperance of my youth, denied, as publicly as possible, merit to all but a few ballads translated from Gaelic writers, or written out of a personal and generally tragic experience.

III

The greater number of those who joined my society had come under the seal of Young Ireland at that age when we are all mere wax; the more ambitious had gone daily to some public library to read the bound volumes of Thomas Davis's old newspaper, and tried to see the world as Davis saw it. No philosophic speculation, no economic question of the day, disturbed an orthodoxy which, unlike that of religion had no philosophic history, and the religious bigot was glad that it should be so. Some few of the younger men were impatient, and it was these younger men, more numerous in the London than in the Dublin Society, who gave me support; and we had been joined by a few older men, some personal friends of my own or my father, who had only historical interest in Thomas Davis and his school. Young Ireland's prose had been as much occupied with Irish virtue, and more with the invader's vices, than its poetry, and we were soon mired and sunk into such problems as to whether Cromwell was altogether black, the heads of the old Irish clans altogether white, the Danes mere robbers and church burners (they tell me at Rosses Point that the Danes keep to this day the maps of the Rosses fields they were driven out of in the 9th century, and plot their return) and as to whether we were or were not once the greatest orators in the world. All the past had been turned into a melodrama with Ireland for blameless hero and poet, novelist and historian had but one object, that we should hiss the villain, and only a minority doubted that the greater the talent the greater the hiss. It was all the harder to substitute for that melodrama a nobler form of art, because there really had been, however different in their form, villain and victim; yet fight that rancour I must, and if I had not made some head against it in 1892 and 1893 it might have silenced in 1907 John Synge, the greatest dramatic genius of Ireland. I am writing of disputes that happened many years ago, that led in later years to much bitterness, and I may exaggerate their immediate importance and violence, but I think I am right in saying that disputes about the merits of Young Ireland so often interrupted our discussion of rules, or of the merit of this or that lecturer, and were so aggravated and crossed by the current wrangle between Parnellite and anti-Parnellite that they delayed our public appearance for a year. Other excited persons, doubtless, seeing that we are of a race intemperate of speech, had looked up from their rancours to the dead Lord Mayors upon the wall, superior men whose like we shall not see again, but never, I think, from rancours so seemingly academic. I was preparing the way without knowing it for a great satirist and master of irony, for master works stir vaguely in many before they grow definite in one man's mind, and to help me I had already flitting through my head, jostling other ideas and so not yet established there, a conviction that we should satirize rather than praise, that original virtue arises from the discovery of evil. If we were, as I had dreaded, declamatory, loose, and bragging, we were but the better fitted, that once declared and measured, to create unyielding personality, manner at once cold and passionate, daring long premeditated act; and if bitter beyond all the people of the world, we might yet lie, that too declared and measured, nearest the honeyed comb:

"Like the clangour of a bell   Sweet and harsh, harsh and sweet,   That is how he learnt so well   To take the roses for his meat."

IV

There were others with followers of their own, and too old or indifferent to join our society. Old men who had never accepted Young Ireland, or middle-aged men kept by some family tradition to the school of thought before it arose, to the Ireland of Daniel O'Connell and of Lever and of Thomas Moore, convivial Ireland with the traditional tear and smile. They sang Moore's Melodies, admitted no poetry but his, and resented Young Ireland's political objections to it as much as my generation's objection to its artificial and easy rhythm; one, an old commercial traveller, a Gaelic scholar who kept an erect head and the animal vigour of youth, frequented the houses of our leading men, and would say in a loud voice, "Thomas Moore, sir, is the greatest heroic poet of ancient or modern times." I think it was the Fire Worshippers in Lalla Rookh that he preferred to Homer; or, jealous for the music of the Melodies, denounce Wagner, then at the top of his vogue; "I would run ten miles through a bog to escape him," he would cry. Then there was a maker of tombstones of whom we had heard much but had seen little, an elderly fighting man, lately imprisoned for beating a wine-merchant. A young member of the London society, afterwards librarian to the National University, D. J. O'Donohue, who had published a dictionary of the Irish poets, containing, I think, two thousand names, had come to Dublin and settled there in a fit of patriotism. He had been born in London, and spoke the most Cockney dialect imaginable, and had picked up, probably from London critics, a dislike for the poetry of Thomas Moore. The tombstone maker invited him to tea, and he arrived with a bundle of books, which he laid beside him upon the table. During tea he began expounding that dislike of his; his host was silent, but he went on, for he was an obstinate little man. Presently the tombstone-maker rose, and having said solemnly, "I have never permitted that great poet to be slandered in my presence," seized his guest by the back of the collar, and flung him out into the street, and after that flung out the books one after another. Meanwhile the guest, as he himself told the tale, stood in the middle of the street repeating, "Nice way to treat a man in your own 'ouse."

V

I shared a lodging full of old books and magazines, covered with dirt and dust, with the head of the Fenian Brotherhood, John O'Leary. "In this country," he had said to me, "a man must have upon his side the Church or the Fenians, and you will never have the Church." He had been converted to nationality by the poems of Davis, and he wished for some analogous movement to that of Davis, but he had known men of letters, had been the friend of Whistler, and knew the faults of the old literature. We had made him the President of our Society, and without him I could do nothing, for his long imprisonment and longer exile, his magnificent appearance, and, above all, the fact that he alone had personality, a point of view not made for the crowd's sake, but for self-expression, made him magnetic to my generation. He and I had long been friends, he had stayed with us at Bedford Park, and my father had painted his portrait, but if I had not shared his lodging he would have opposed me. He was an old man, and my point of view was not that of his youth, and it often took me half the day to make him understand, so suspicious he was of all innovation, some simple thing that he would presently support with ardour. He had grown up in a European movement when the revolutionist thought that he, above all men, must appeal to the highest motive, be guided by some ideal principle, be a little like Cato or like Brutus, and he had lived to see the change Dostoievsky examined in The Possessed. Men who had been of his party, and oftener their sons, preached assassination and the bomb; and, worst of all, the majority of his countrymen followed after constitutional politicians who practised opportunism, and had, as he believed, such low morals that they would lie, or publish private correspondence, if it might advance their cause. He would split every practical project into its constituent elements, like a clerical casuist, to find if it might not lead into some moral error; but, were the project revolutionary, he would sometimes temper condemnation with pity. Though he would cast off his oldest acquaintance did he suspect him of rubbing shoulders with some carrier of bombs, I have heard him say of a man who blew himself up in an attempt to blow up Westminster Bridge, "He was not a bad man, but he had too great a moral nature for his intellect, not that he lacked intellect." He did not explain, but he meant, I suppose, that the spectacle of injustice might madden a good man more quickly than some common man. Such men were of his own sort, though gone astray, but the constitutional politicians he had been fighting all his life, and all they did displeased him. It was not that he thought their aim wrong, or that they could not achieve it; he had accepted Gladstone's Home Rule Bill; but that in his eyes they degraded manhood. "If England has been brought to do us justice by such men," he would say, "that is not because of our strength, but because of her weakness." He had a particular hatred for the rush of emotion that followed the announcement of Gladstone's conversion, for what was called "The Union of Hearts," and derided its sentimentality; "Nations may respect one another," he would say, "they cannot love." His ancestors had probably kept little shops, or managed little farms in County Tipperary, yet he hated democracy, though he never used the word either for praise or blame, with more than feudal hatred. "No gentleman can be a socialist," he said, and then, with a thoughtful look, "He might be an anarchist." He had no philosophy, but things distressed his palate, and two of those things were International propaganda and the Organised State, and Socialism aimed at both, nor could he speak such words as "philanthropy," "humanitarianism," without showing by his tone of voice that they offended him. The Church pleased him little better; there was an old Fenian quarrel there, and he would say, "My religion is the old Persian, to pull the bow and tell the truth." He had no self-consciousness, no visible pride, and would have hated anything that could have been called a gesture, was indeed scarce artist enough to invent a gesture; yet he would never speak of the hardship of his prison life, though abundantly enough of its humours, and once, when I pressed him, replied, "I was in the hands of my enemy, why should I complain?" A few years ago I heard that the Governor of the prison had asked why he did not report some unnecessary discomfort, and O'Leary had said, "I did not come here to complain." Now that he is dead, I wish that I could question him, and perhaps discover whether in early youth he had come across some teacher who had expounded Roman virtue, but I doubt if I would have learnt anything, for I think the wax had long forgotten the seal, if seal there were. The seal was doubtless made before the eloquent humanitarian 'forties and 'fifties, and was one kind with that that had moulded the youthful mind of Savage Landor. Stephens, the founder of Fenianism, had discovered him searching the second-hand bookstalls for rare editions, and enrolled him in his organization. "You have no chance of success," O'Leary had said "but it will be good for the morale of the country" (morale was his great word), "and I will join on the condition that I am never asked to enrol anybody." He still searched the second-hand bookstalls, and had great numbers of books, especially of Irish history and literature, and when I, exhausted over our morning's casuistry, would sit down to my day's work (I was writing The Secret Rose) he would make his tranquil way to the Dublin Quays. In the evening, over his coffee, he would write passages for his memoirs upon postcards and odd scraps of paper, taking immense trouble with every word and comma, for the great work must be a masterpiece of style. When it was finished, it was unreadable, being dry, abstract, and confused; no picture had ever passed before his mind's eye. He was a victim, I think, of a movement where opinions stick men together, or keep them apart, like a kind of bird lime, and without any relation to their natural likes and tastes, and where men of rich nature must give themselves up to an irritation which they no longer recognise because it is always present. I often wonder why he gave me his friendship, why it was he who found almost all the subscribers for my Wanderings of Usheen, and why he now supported me in all I did, for how could he like verses that were all picture, all emotion, all association, all mythology? He could not have approved my criticism either, for I exalted Mask and Image above the 18th century logic which he loved, and set experience before observation, emotion before fact. Yet he would say, "I have only three followers, Taylor, Yeats, and Rolleston," and presently he cast out Rolleston, "Davitt wants to convert thousands, but I want two or three." I think that perhaps it was because he no more wished to strengthen Irish Nationalism by second-rate literature than by second-rate morality, and was content that we agreed in that. "There are things a man must not do to save a Nation," he had once told me, and when I asked what things, had said, "To cry in public," and I think it probable that he would have added, if pressed, "To write oratorical or insincere verse."

O'Leary's movements and intonations were full of impulse, but John F. Taylor's voice in private discussion had no emotional quality except in the expression of scorn; if he moved an arm it moved from the shoulder or elbow alone, and when he walked he moved from the waist only, and seemed an automaton, a wooden soldier, as if he had no life that was not dry and abstract. Except at moments of public oratory, he lacked all personality, though when one saw him respectful and gentle with O'Leary, as with some charming woman, one saw that he felt its fascination. In letters, or in painting, it repelled him unless it were harsh and obvious, and, therefore, though his vast erudition included much art and letters, he lacked artistic feeling, and judged everything by the moral sense. He had great ambition, and had he joined some established party, or found some practicable policy, he might have been followed, might have produced even some great effect, but he must have known that in defeat no man would follow him, as they followed O'Leary, as they followed Parnell. His oratory was noble, strange, even beautiful, at moments the greatest I have ever listened to; but, the speech over, where there had been, as it seemed, so little of himself, all coming from beyond himself, we saw precisely as before an ungainly body in unsuitable, badly-fitting clothes, and heard an excited voice speaking ill of this man or that other. We knew that he could never give us that one price we would accept, that he would never find a practicable policy; that no party would admit, no government negotiate with, a man notorious for a temper, that, if it gave him genius, could at times carry him to the edge of insanity.

Born in some country town, the son of some little watchmaker, he had been a shop assistant, put himself to college and the bar, learned to speak at temperance meetings and Young Ireland societies, and was now a Queen's Counsel famous for his defence of country criminals, whose cases had seemed hopeless, Taylor's boys, their neighbours called them or they called themselves. He had shaped his style and his imagination from Carlyle, the chief inspirer of self-educated men in the 'eighties and early 'nineties. "I prefer Emerson's Oversoul," the Condalkin cobbler said to me, "but I always read Carlyle when I am wild with the neighbours"; but he used his master's style, as Mitchell had done before, to abase what his master loved, to exalt what his master scorned. His historical erudition seemed as vast as that of York Powell, but his interests were not Powell's, for he had no picture before the mind's eye, and had but one object, a plea of not guilty, entered in his country's name before a jury which he believed to be packed. O'Leary cared nothing for his country's glory, its individuality alone seemed important in his eyes; he was like some man, who serves a woman all his life without asking whether she be good or bad, wise or foolish; but Taylor cared for nothing else; he was so much O'Leary's disciple that he would say in conversation, "We are demoralised, what case for change if we are not?" for O'Leary admitted no ground for reform outside the moral life, but when he spoke to the great plea he would make no admission. He spoke to it in the most obscure places, in little halls in back streets where the white-washed walls are foul with grease from many heads, before some audience of medical students or of shop assistants, for he was like a man under a curse, compelled to hide his genius, and compelled to show in conspicuous places his ill judgment and his temper.

His distaste for myself, broken by occasional tolerance, in so far as it was not distaste for an imagination that seemed to him aesthetic rather than ethical, was because I had published Irish folk-lore in English reviews to the discredit, as he thought, of the Irish peasantry, and because, England within earshot, I found fault with the Young Ireland prose and poetry. He would have hated The Playboy of the Western World, and his death a little before its performance was fortunate for Synge and myself. His articles are nothing, and his one historical work, a life of Hugh O'Neill, is almost nothing, lacking the living voice; and now, though a most formidable man, he is forgotten, but for the fading memory of a few friends, and for what an enemy has written here and elsewhere. Did not Leonardo da Vinci warn the imaginative man against pre-occupation with arts that cannot survive his death?

VI

When Carleton was dying in 1870, he said there would be nothing more about Irish Literature for twenty years, and his words were fulfilled, for the land war had filled Ireland with its bitterness; but imagination had begun to stir again. I had the same confidence in the future that Lady Gregory and I had eight or nine years later, when we founded an Irish Theatre, though there were neither, as it seemed, plays or players. There were already a few known men to start my popular series, and to keep it popular until the men, whose names I did not know, had learnt to express themselves. I had met Dr. Douglas Hyde when I lived in Dublin, and he was still an undergraduate. I have a memory of meeting in college rooms for the first time a very dark young man, who filled me with surprise, partly because he had pushed a snuffbox towards me, and partly because there was something about his vague serious eyes, as in his high cheek bones, that suggested a different civilization, a different race. I had set him down as a peasant, and wondered what brought him to college, and to a Protestant college, but somebody explained that he belonged to some branch of the Hydes of Castle Hyde, and that he had a Protestant Rector for father. He had much frequented the company of old countrymen, and had so acquired the Irish language, and his taste for snuff, and for moderate quantities of a detestable species of illegal whiskey distilled from the potato by certain of his neighbours. He had already, though intellectual Dublin knew nothing of it, considerable popularity as a Gaelic poet, mowers and reapers singing his songs from Donegal to Kerry. Years afterwards I was to stand at his side and listen to Galway mowers singing his Gaelic words without knowing whose words they sang. It is so in India, where peasants sing the words of the great poet of Bengal without knowing whose words they sing, and it must often be so where the old imaginative folk life is undisturbed, and it is so amongst schoolboys who hand their story books to one another without looking at the title page to read the author's name. Here and there, however, the peasants had not lost the habit of Gaelic criticism, picked up, perhaps, from the poets who took refuge among them after the ruin of the great Catholic families, from men like that O'Rahilly, who cries in a translation from the Gaelic that is itself a masterpiece of concentrated passion

"The periwinkle and the tough dog-fish
Towards evening time have got into my dish."

An old rascal was kept in food and whiskey for a fortnight by some Connaught village under the belief that he was Craoibhin Aoibhin, "the pleasant little branch," as Doctor Hyde signed himself in the newspapers where the villagers had found his songs. The impostor's thirst only strengthened belief in his genius, for the Gaelic song-writers have had the infirmities of Robert Burns, "It is not the drink but the company," one of the last has sung. Since that first meeting Doctor Hyde and I had corresponded, and he had sent me in manuscript the best tale in my Faery and Folk Tales, and I think I had something to do with the London publication of his Beside the Fire, a book written in the beautiful English of Connaught, which is Gaelic in idiom and Tudor in vocabulary, and indeed, the first book to use it in the expression of emotion and romance, for Carleton and his school had turned it into farce. Henley had praised him, and York Powell had said, "If he goes on as he has begun, he will be the greatest folk-loreist who has ever lived"; and I know no first book of verse of our time that is at once so romantic and so concrete as his Gaelic Abhla de'n Craoibh; but in a few years Dublin was to laugh him, or rail him, out of his genius. He had no critical capacity, having indeed for certain years the uncritical folk-genius, as no educated Irish or Englishman has ever had it, writing out of an imitative sympathy like that of a child catching a tune and leaving it to chance to call the tune; and the failure of our first attempt to create a modern Irish literature permitted the ruin of that genius. He was to create a great popular movement, far more important in its practical results than any movement I could have made, no matter what my luck, but, being neither quarrelsome nor vain, he will not be angry if I say, for the sake of those who come after us, that I mourn for the "greatest folk-loreist who ever lived," and for the great poet who died in his youth. The Harps and Pepperpots got him and the Harps and Pepperpots kept him till he wrote in our common English, "It must be either English or Irish," said some patriotic editor, Young Ireland practice in his head that needs such sifting that he who would write it vigorously must write it like a learned language, and took for his model the newspaper upon his breakfast table, and became for no base reason beloved by multitudes who should never have heard his name till their schoolmasters showed it upon his tomb. That very incapacity for criticism made him the cajoler of crowds, and of individual men and women; "He should not be in the world at all," said one admiring elderly woman, "or doing the world's work"; and for certain years young Irish women were to display his pseudonym, "Craoibhin Aoibhin," in gilt letters upon their hat bands.

"Dear Craoibhin Aoibhin,......impart to us, We'll keep the secret, a new trick to please; Is there a bridle for this Proteus That turns and changes like his draughty seas, Or is there none, most popular of men, But, when they mock us, that we mock again?"

VII

Standish O'Grady, upon the other hand, was at once all passion and all judgment. And yet those who knew him better than I assured me he could find quarrel in a straw; and I did know that he had quarrelled a few years back with Jack Nettleship. Nettleship's account had been, "My mother cannot endure the God of the Old Testament, but likes Jesus Christ; whereas I like the God of the Old Testament, and cannot endure Jesus Christ; and we have got into the way of quarrelling about it at lunch; and once, when O'Grady lunched with us, he said it was the most disgraceful spectacle he had ever seen, and walked out." Indeed, I wanted him among my writers, because of his quarrels, for, having much passion and little rancour, the more he quarrelled, the nobler, the more patched with metaphor, the more musical his style became, and if he were in his turn attacked, he knew a trick of speech that made us murmur, "We do it wrong, being so majestical, to offer it the show of violence." Sometimes he quarrelled most where he loved most. A Unionist in politics, a leader-writer on The Daily Express, the most Conservative paper in Ireland, hater of every form of democracy, he had given all his heart to the smaller Irish landowners, to whom he belonged, and with whom his childhood had been spent, and for them he wrote his books, and would soon rage over their failings in certain famous passages that many men would repeat to themselves like poets' rhymes. All round us people talked or wrote for victory's sake, and were hated for their victories, but here was a man whose rage was a swan-song over all that he had held most dear, and to whom for that very reason every Irish imaginative writer owed a portion of his soul. In his unfinished History of Ireland he had made the old Irish heroes, Fion, and Oisin, and Cuchullan, alive again, taking them, for I think he knew no Gaelic, from the dry pages of O'Curry and his school, and condensing and arranging, as he thought Homer would have arranged and condensed. Lady Gregory has told the same tales, but keeping closer to the Gaelic text, and with greater powers of arrangement and a more original style, but O'Grady was the first, and we had read him in our 'teens. I think that, had I succeeded, a popular audience could have changed him little, and that his genius would have stayed, as it had been shaped by his youth in some provincial society, and that to the end he would have shown his best in occasional thrusts and parries. But I do think that if, instead of that one admirable little book The Bog of Stars, we had got all his histories and imaginative works into the hands of our young men, he might have brought the imagination of Ireland nearer the Image and the honeycomb.

Lionel Johnson was to be our critic, and above all our theologian, for he had been converted to Catholicism, and his orthodoxy, too learned to question, had accepted all that we did, and most of our plans. Historic Catholicism, with all its counsels and its dogmas, stirred his passion like the beauty of a mistress, and the unlearned parish priests who thought good literature or good criticism dangerous were in his eyes "all heretics." He belonged to a family that had called itself Irish some generations back, and its recent English generations but enabled him to see as one single sacred tradition Irish nationality and Catholic religion. How should he fail to know the Holy Land? Had he not been in Egypt? He had joined our London Irish Literary Society, attended its committee meetings, and given lectures in London, in Dublin, and in Belfast, on Irish novelists and Irish poetry, reading his lectures always, and yet affecting his audience as I, with my spoken lectures, could not, perhaps because Ireland had still the shape it had received from the eighteenth century, and so felt the dignity, not the artifice, of his elaborate periods. He was very little, and at a first glance he seemed but a schoolboy of fifteen. I remember saying one night at the Rhymers', when he spoke of passing safely, almost nightly, through Seven Dials, then a dangerous neighbourhood, "Who would expect to find anything in your pockets but a pegtop and a piece of string?" But one never thought of his small stature when he spoke or read. He had the delicate strong features of a certain filleted head of a Greek athlete in the British Museum, an archaistic Graeco-Roman copy of a masterpiece of the fourth century, and that resemblance seemed symbolic of the austere nobility of his verse. He was now in his best years, writing with great ease and power; neither I, nor, I think, any other, foresaw his tragedy.

He suffered from insomnia, and some doctor, while he was still at the University, had recommended alcohol, and he had, in a vain hope of sleep, increased the amount, as Rossetti had increased his doses of chloral, and now he drank for drinking's sake. He drank a great deal too much, and, though nothing could, it seemed, disturb his calm or unsteady his hand or foot, his doctrine, after a certain number of glasses, would become more ascetic, more contemptuous of all that we call human life. I have heard him, after four or five glasses of wine, praise some church father who freed himself from sexual passion by a surgical operation, and deny with scorn, and much historical evidence, that a gelded man lost anything of intellectual power. Even without stimulant his theology conceded nothing to human weakness, and I can remember his saying with energy, "I wish those people who deny the eternity of punishment could realise their unspeakable vulgarity."

Now that I know his end, I see him creating, to use a favourite adjective of his, "marmorean" verse, and believing the most terrible doctrines to keep down his own turbulence. One image of that stay in Dublin is so clear before me that it has blotted out most other images of that time. He is sitting at a lodging-house table, which I have just left at three in the morning, and round him lie or sit in huddled attitudes half-a-dozen men in various states of intoxication: and he is looking straight before him with head erect, and one hand resting upon the table. As I reach the stairs I hear him say, in a clear, unshaken voice, "I believe in nothing but the Holy Roman Catholic Church." He sometimes spoke of drink as something which he could put aside at any moment, and his friends believed, and I think he liked us to believe, that he would shortly enter a monastery. Did he deceive us deliberately? Did he himself already foresee the moment when he would write The Dark Angel? I am almost certain that he did, for he had already written Mystic and Cavalier, where the historical setting is, I believe, but masquerade.

"Go from me: I am one of those, who fall.
What! hath no cold wind swept your heart at all,
In my sad company? Before the end,
Go from me, dear my friend!

Yours are the victories of light: your feet
Rest from good toil, where rest is brave and sweet.
But after warfare in a mourning gloom
I rest in clouds of doom.

Seek with thine eyes to pierce this crystal sphere:
Canst read a fate there, prosperous and clear?

Only the mists, only the weeping clouds:
Dimness, and airy shrouds.

O rich and sounding voices of the air!
Interpreters and prophets of despair:
Priests of a fearful sacrament! I come
To make with you my home."

VIII

Sir Charles Gavan Duffy arrived. He brought with him much manuscript, the private letters of a
Young Ireland poetess, a dry but informing unpublished historical essay by Davis, and an
unpublished novel by William Carleton, into the middle of which he had dropped a hot coal, so that
nothing remained but the borders of every page. He hired a young man to read him, after dinner,
Carlyle's Heroes and Hero-Worship, and before dinner was gracious to all our men of authority and
especially to our Harps and Pepperpots. Taylor compared him to Odysseus returning to Ithaca, and
every newspaper published his biography. He was a white-haired old man, who had written the
standard history of Young Ireland, had emigrated to Australia, had been the first Australian
Federalist, and later Prime Minister, but, in all his writings, in which there is so much honesty, so
little rancour, there is not one sentence that has any meaning when separated from its place in
argument or narrative, not one distinguished because of its thought or music. One imagined his
youth in some little gaunt Irish town, where no building or custom is revered for its antiquity; and
there speaking a language where no word, even in solitude, is ever spoken slowly and carefully
because of emotional implication; and of his manhood of practical politics, of the dirty piece of
orange-peel in the corner of the stairs as one climbs up to some newspaper office; of public
meetings where it would be treacherous amid so much geniality to speak, or even to think of
anything that might cause a moment's misunderstanding in one's own party. No argument of mine
was intelligible to him, and I would have been powerless, but that fifty years ago he had made an
enemy, and though that enemy was long dead, his school remained. He had attacked, why or with
what result I do not remember, the only Young Ireland politician who had music and personality,
though rancorous and devil-possessed. At some public meeting of ours, where he spoke amid great
applause, in smooth, Gladstonian periods, of his proposed Irish publishing firm, one heard faint
hostile murmurs, and at last a voice cried, "Remember Newry," and a voice answered, "There is a
grave there!" and a part of the audience sang, "Here's to John Mitchell that is gone, boys, gone;
Here's to the friends that are gone." The meeting over, a group of us, indignant that the meeting we
had called for his welcome should have contained those malcontents, gathered about him to
apologize. He had written a pamphlet, he explained: he would give us copies. We would see that he
was in the right, how badly Mitchell had behaved. But in Ireland personality, if it be but harsh and
hard, has lovers, and some of us, I think, may have gone home muttering, "How dare he be in the
right if Mitchell is in the wrong?"

IX

He wanted "to complete the Young Ireland movement", to do all that had been left undone because
of the Famine, or the death of Davis, or his own emigration; and all the younger men were upon my
side in resisting that. They might not want the books I wanted, but they did want books written by
their own generation, and we began to struggle with him over the control of the company. Taylor
became very angry, and I can understand what I looked like in his eyes, when I remember Edwin

Ellis's seriously-intended warning, "It is bad manners for a man under thirty to permit himself to be in the right." But John O'Leary supported me throughout.

When Gavin Duffy had gone to London to draw up articles of association for his company, for which he had found many shareholders in Dublin, the dispute became very fierce. One night members of the general public climbed the six flights of stairs to our committee room, now no longer in the Mansion House, and found seats for themselves just behind our chairs. We were all too angry to send them away, or even to notice their presence, for I was accused of saying at a public meeting in Cork, "Our books," when I should have said, "Sir Charles Gavan Duffy's books." I was not Taylor's match with the spoken word, and barely matched him with the written word. At twenty-seven or twenty-eight I was immature and clumsy, and O'Leary's support was capricious, for, being but a spectator of life, he would desert me if I used a bad argument, and would not return till I found a good one; and our chairman, Dr. Hyde, "most popular of men," sat dreaming of his old white cockatoo in far-away Roscommon. Our very success had been a misfortune, for an opposition which had been literary and political, now that it had spread to the general public, brought religious prejudice to its aid. Suddenly, when the company seemed all but established, and a scheme had been thought out which gave some representation on its governing board to contemporary Irish writers, Gavan Duffy produced a letter from Archbishop Walsh, and threw the project up. The letter had warned him that after his death the company would fall under a dangerous influence. At this moment the always benevolent friend, to whom I had explained in confidence, when asking his support, my arrangements with my publisher, went to Gavan Duffy and suggested that they should together offer Mr Fisher Unwin a series of Irish books, and Mr Fisher Unwin and his reader accepted the series under the belief that it was my project that they accepted. I went to London to find the contract signed, and that all I could do was to get two sub-editors appointed, responsible to the two societies. Two or three good books were published, especially Dr. Hyde's Short History of Gaelic Literature, and Standish O'Grady's Bog of Stars; but the series was killed by its first volume, Thomas Davis's dry but informing historical essay. So important had our movement seemed that ten thousand copies had been sold before anybody had time to read it, and then came a dead stop.

Gavan Duffy knew nothing of my plans, and so was guiltless, and my friend had heard me discuss many things that evening. I had perhaps dispraised the humanitarian Stephen Phillips, already in his first vogue, and praised Francis Thompson, but half-rescued from his gutter; or flouted his belief in the perpetual marriage of genius and virtue by numbering the vices of famous men; this man's venery, that man's drink. He could not be expected to remember that where I had said so much of no account, I said one thing, and he had made no reply, that I thought of great account. He died a few months ago, and it would have surprised and shocked him if any man had told him that he was unforgiven; had he not forgotten all about it long ago? A German doctor has said that if we leave an umbrella at a friend's house it is because we have a sub-conscious desire to re-visit that house; and he had perhaps a sub-conscious desire that my too tumultuous generation should not have its say.

X

I was at Sligo when I received a letter from John O'Leary, saying that I could do no more in Dublin, for even the younger men had turned against me, were "jealous," his letter said, though what they had to be jealous of God knows. He said further that it was all my own fault, that he had warned me what would happen if I lived on terms of intimacy with those I tried to influence. I should have kept myself apart and alone. It was all true; through some influence from an earlier generation, from Walt Whitman, perhaps, I had sat talking in public bars, had talked late into the night at many men's houses, showing all my convictions to men that were but ready for one, and used conversation to explore and discover among men who looked for authority. I did not yet know that intellectual freedom and social equality are incompatible; and yet, if I had, could hardly have lived otherwise, being too young for silence. The trouble came from half a dozen obscure young men, who having nothing to do attended every meeting and were able to overturn a project, that seemed my only bridge to other projects, including a travelling theatre. We had planned small libraries of Irish literature in connection with our country branches; we collected books and money, sending a lecturer to every branch and taking half the proceeds of that lecture to buy books. Maud Gonne, whose beauty could draw a great audience in any country town, had been the lecturer. The scheme was very nearly self-supporting, and six or seven bundles of books, chosen after much disputation by John O'Leary, J. F. Taylor, and myself, had been despatched to some six or seven branches. "The country will support this work" Taylor had said somewhere on some public platform, "because we are the most inflammable people on God's earth," his harsh voice giving almost a quality of style to Carlylian commonplace; but we are also a very jealous people. The half-a-dozen young men, if a little jealous of me, were still more jealous of those country branches which were getting so much notice, and where there was so much of that peasant mind their schoolmasters had taught them to despise. One must be English or Irish, they would have said. I returned to find a great box of books appropriated for some Dublin purpose and the whole scheme abandoned. I know that it was a bitter moment because I remember with gratitude words spoken not to my ear, but for my ear, by a young man who had lately joined our Society, Mr. Stephen McKenna, now well-known amongst scholars for his distinguished translations of Plotinus, and I seem to remember that I lost through anger what gift of persuasion I may possess, and that I was all the more helpless because I felt that even the best of us disagreed about everything at heart. I began to feel that I needed a hostess more than a society, but that I was not to find for years to come. I tried to persuade Maud Gonne to be that hostess, but her social life was in Paris, and she had already formed a new ambition, the turning of French public opinion against England. Without intellectual freedom there can be no agreement, and in Nationalist Dublin there was not, indeed there still is not, any society where a man is heard by the right ears, but never overheard by the wrong, and where he speaks his whole mind gaily, and is not the cautious husband of a part; where phantasy can play before matured into conviction; where life can shine and ring, and lack utility. Mere life lacking the protection of wealth or rank, or some beauty's privilege of caprice cannot choose its company, taking up and dropping men merely because it likes, or dislikes, their manners and their looks, and in its stead opinion crushes and rends, and all is hatred and bitterness: wheel biting upon wheel, a roar of steel or iron tackle, a mill of argument grinding all things down to mediocrity. If, as I think, minds and metals correspond the goldsmiths of Paris foretold the French Revolution when they substituted steel for that unserviceable gold in the manufacture of the more expensive jewel work, and made those large, flat steel buttons for men of fashion whereby the card players were able to cheat by studying the reflections of the cards.

XI

No country could have more natural distaste for equality, for in every circle there was some man ridiculous for posing as the type of some romantic or distinguished quality. One of our friends, a man of talent and of learning, whose ancestors had come, he believed, from Denmark in the ninth century, looked and talked the distinguished foreigner so perfectly that a patriotic newspaper gave particulars of his supposed relations in contemporary Denmark! A half-mad old man who had served for a few months in the Pope's army, many years before, still rode an old white warhorse in all national processions, and, if their enemies were not lying, one Town Councillor had challenged another to a duel by flinging his glove upon the floor; while a popular Lord Mayor had boasted in a public speech that he never went to bed at night without reading at least twelve pages of Sappho. Then, too, in those conversations of the small hours, to which O'Leary had so much objected, whenever we did not speak of art and letters, we spoke of Parnell. We told each other that he had admitted no man to his counsel; that when some member of his party found himself in the same hotel by chance, that member would think to stay there a presumption, and move to some other lodging; and, above all, we spoke of his pride, that made him hide all emotion while before his enemy. Once he had seemed callous and indifferent to the House of Commons, Foster had accused him of abetting assassination, but when he came among his followers his hands were full of blood, because he had torn them with his nails. What excitement there would have been, what sense of mystery would have stirred all our hearts, and stirred hearts all through the country, where there was still, and for many years to come, but one overmastering topic, had we known the story Mrs. Parnell tells of that scene on Brighton Pier. He and the woman that he loved stood there upon a night of storm, when his power was at its greatest height, and still unthreatened. He caught her from the ground and held her at arm's length out over the water and she lay there motionless, knowing that, had she moved, he would have drowned himself and her. Perhaps unmotived self-immolation, were that possible, or else at mere suggestion of storm and night, were as great evidence as such a man could give of power over self, and so of the expression of the self.

XII

When I look back upon my Irish propaganda of those years I can see little but its bitterness. I never met with, or but met to quarrel with, my father's old family acquaintance; or with acquaintance I myself might have found, and kept, among the prosperous educated class, who had all the great appointments at University or Castle; and this I did by deliberate calculation. If I must attack so much that seemed sacred to Irish nationalist opinion, I must, I knew, see to it that no man suspect me of doing it to flatter Unionist opinion. Whenever I got the support of some man who belonged by birth and education to University or Castle, I would say, "Now you must be baptized of the gutter." I chose Royal visits especially for demonstrations of disloyalty, rolling up with my own hands the red carpet spread by some elderly Nationalist, softened or weakened by time, to welcome Viceroyalty; and threatening, if the London Society drank to the King's health, that my friends and I would demonstrate against it by turning our glasses upside down; and was presently to discover that one can grow impassioned and fanatical about opinions, which one has chosen as one might choose a side upon the football field; and I thought many a time of the pleasant Dublin houses that would never ask me to dine; and the still pleasanter houses with trout-streams near at hand, that would never ask me upon a visit. I became absurdly sensitive, glancing about me in certain public places, the private view of our Academy, or the like, to discover imagined enemies; and even now, after twenty or thirty years, I feel at times that I have not recovered my natural manner. Yet it was in those pleasant houses, among the young men and the young girls, that we were to make our converts. When we loathe ourselves or our world, if that loathing but turn to intellect, we see self or world and its anti-self as in one vision; when loathing remains but loathing, world or self consumes itself away, and we turn to its mechanical opposite. Popular Nationalism and Unionism so changed into one another, being each but the other's headache. The Nationalist abstractions were like the fixed ideas of some hysterical woman, a part of the mind turned into stone, and all the rest a seething and burning; and Unionist Ireland had re-acted from that seething and burning to a cynical indifference, and from those fixed ideas to whatever might bring the most easy and obvious success.

I remember Taylor at some public debate, stiff of body and tense of voice; and the contrasting figure of Fitzgibbon, the Lord Justice of Appeal of the moment and his calm, flowing sentences, satisfactory to hear and impossible to remember. Taylor speaks of a little nation of antiquity, which he does not name, "set between the great Empire of Persia and the great Empire of Rome." Into the mouths of those great Empires he puts the arguments of Fitzgibbon, and such as he, "Join with our greatness! What in comparison to that is your little, beggarly nationality?" And then I recall the excitement, the shiver of the nerves, as his voice rose to an ecstatic cry, "Out of that nation came the salvation of the world." I remember, too, and grow angry, as it were yesterday, a letter from that Lord Justice of

Appeal, who had changed his politics for advancement's sake, recommending a correspondent to avoid us, because we dissuaded people from the study of "Shakespeare and Kingsley."

Edward Dowden, my father's old friend, with his dark romantic face, the one man of letters Dublin Unionism possessed, was withering in that barren soil. Towards the end of his life he confessed to a near friend that he would have wished before all things to have been the lover of many women; and some careless lecture, upon the youthful Goethe, had in early life drawn down upon him the displeasure of the Protestant Archbishop. And yet he turned Shakespeare into a British Benthamite, flattered Shelley but to hide his own growing lack of sympathy, abandoned for like reason that study of Goethe that should have been his life-work, and at last cared but for Wordsworth, the one great poet who, after brief blossom, was cut and sawn into planks of obvious utility. I called upon him from time to time out of gratitude for old encouragements, and because, among the Dublin houses open to me, his alone was pleasant to the eye, with its many books and its air of scholarship. But when O'Grady had declared, rancorous for once but under substantial provocation, that he had "a bad head and a worse heart," I found my welcome troubled and called no more.

XIII

The one house where nobody thought or talked politics was a house in Ely Place, where a number of young men lived together, and, for want of a better name, were called Theosophists. Beside the resident members, other members dropped in and out during the day, and the reading-room was a place of much discussion about philosophy and about the arts. The house had been taken in the name of the engineer to the Board of Works, a black-bearded young man, with a passion for Manichean philosophy, and all accepted him as host; and sometimes the conversation, especially when I was there, became too ghostly for the nerves of his young and delicate wife, and he would be made angry. I remember young men struggling, with inexact terminology and insufficient learning, for some new religious conception, on which they could base their lives; and some few strange or able men.

At the top of the house lived a medical student who read Plato and took haschisch, and a young Scotchman who owned a vegetarian restaurant, and had just returned from America, where he had gone as the disciple of the Prophet Harris, and where he would soon return in the train of some new prophet. When one asked what set him on his wanderings, he told of a young Highlander, his friend in boyhood, whose cap was always plucked off at a certain twist in the road, till the fathers of the village fastened it upon his head by recommending drink and women. When he had gone, his room was inherited by an American hypnotist, who had lived among the Zuni Indians with the explorer Cushant, and told of a Zuni Indian who, irritated by some white man's praise of telephone and telegraph, cried out, "Can they do that?" and cast above his head two handfuls of sand that burst into flame, and flamed till his head seemed wrapped in fire. He professed to talk the philosophy of the Zuni Indians, but it seemed to me the vague Platonism that all there talked, except that he spoke much of men passing in sleep into the heart of mountains; a doctrine that was presently incorporated in the mythology of the house, to send young men and women hither and thither inquiring for sacred places. On a lower floor lived a strange red-haired girl, all whose thoughts were set upon painting and poetry, conceived as abstract images like Love and Penury in the Symposium; and to these images she sacrificed herself with Asiatic fanaticism. The engineer had discovered her starving somewhere in an unfurnished or half-furnished room, and that she had lived for many weeks upon bread and shell-cocoa, so that her food never cost her more than a penny a day. Born into a county family, who were so haughty that their neighbours called them the Royal Family, she had quarrelled with a mad father, who had never, his tenants declared, "unscrewed the top of his flask with any man," because she wished to study art, had ran away from home, had lived for a time by selling her watch, and then by occasional stories in an Irish paper. For some weeks she had paid half-a-crown a week to some poor woman to see her to the art schools and back, for she considered it wrong for a woman to show herself in public places unattended; but of late she had been unable to afford the school fees. The engineer engaged her as a companion for his wife, and gave her money enough to begin her studies once more. She had talent and imagination, a gift for style; but, though ready to face death for painting and poetry, conceived as allegorical figures, she hated her own genius, and had not met praise and sympathy early enough to overcome the hatred. Face to face with paint and canvas, pen and paper, she saw nothing of her genius but its cruelty, and would have scarce arrived before she would find some excuse to leave the schools for the day, if indeed she had not invented over her breakfast some occupation so laborious that she could call it a duty, and so not go at all. Most watched her in mockery, but I watched in sympathy; composition strained my nerves and spoiled my sleep; and yet, as far back as I could trace, and in Ireland we have long memories, my paternal ancestors had worked at some intellectual pursuit, while hers had shot and hunted. She could at any time, had she given up her profession, which her father had raged against, not because it was art, but because it was a profession, have returned to the common comfortable life of women. When, a little later, she had quarrelled with the engineer or his wife, and gone back to bread and shell-cocoa I brought her an offer from some Dublin merchant of fairly well paid advertisement work, which would have been less laborious than artistic creation; but she said that to draw advertisements was to degrade art, thanked me elaborately, and did not disguise her indignation. She had, I believe, returned to starvation with joy, for constant anaemia would shortly give her an argument strong enough to silence her conscience when the allegorical images glared upon her, and, apart from that, starvation and misery had a large share in her ritual of worship.

XIV

At the top of the house and at the time I remember best, in the same room with the young Scotchman, lived Mr. George Russell (A.E.), and the house and the society were divided into his adherents and those of the engineer; and I heard of some quarrelling between the factions. The rivalry was sub-conscious. Neither had willingly opposed the other in any matter of importance. The engineer had all the financial responsibility, and George Russell was, in the eyes of the community, saint and genius. Had either seen that the question at issue was the leadership of mystical thought in Dublin, he would, I think, have given way, but the dispute seemed trivial. At the weekly meetings, anything might be discussed; no chairman called a speaker to order; an atheistic workman could denounce religion, or a pious Catholic confound theosophy with atheism; and the engineer, precise and practical, disapproved. He had an object. He wished to make converts for a definite form of belief, and here an enemy, if a better speaker, might make all the converts. He wished to confine discussion to members of the society, and had proposed in committee, I was told, a resolution on the subject; while Russell, who had refused to join my National Literary Society, because the party of Harp and Pepperpot had set limits to discussion, resisted, and at last defeated him. In a couple of years some new dispute arose; he resigned, and founded a society which drew doctrine and method from America or London; and Russell became, as he is to-day, the one masterful influence among young Dublin men and women who love religious speculation, but have no historical faith.

When Russell and I had been at the Art School six or seven years before, he had been almost unintelligible. He had seemed incapable of coherent thought, and perhaps was so at certain moments. The idea came upon him, he has told me, that, if he spoke he would reveal that he had lost coherence; and for the three days that the idea lasted spent the hours of daylight wandering upon the Dublin mountains, that he might escape the necessity for speech. I used to listen to him at that time, mostly walking through the streets at night, for the sake of some stray sentence, beautiful and profound, amid many words that seemed without meaning; and there were others, too, who walked and listened, for he had become, I think, to all his fellow students, sacred, as the fool is sacred in the East. We copied the model laboriously, but he would draw without research into the natural form, and call his study "St. John in the Wilderness"; but I can remember the almost scared look and the half-whisper of a student, now a successful sculptor, who said, pointing to the modelling of a shoulder, "That is too easy, a great deal too easy!" For with brush and pencil he was too coherent.

We derided each other, told absurd tales to one another's discredit, but we never derided him, or told tales to his discredit. He stood outside the sense of comedy his friend John Eglinton has called "the social cement" of our civilization; and we would "gush" when we spoke of him, as men do when they praise something incomprehensible. But when he painted there was no difficulty in comprehending. How could that ease and rapidity of composition, so far beyond anything that we could attain to, belong to a man whose words seemed often without meaning?

A few months before I had come to Ireland he had sent me some verses, which I had liked till Edwin Ellis had laughed me from my liking by proving that no line had a rhythm that agreed with any other, and that, the moment one thought he had settled upon some scheme of rhyme, he would break from it without reason. But now his verse was clear in thought and delicate in form. He wrote without premeditation or labour. It had, as it were, organized itself, and grown as nervous and living as if it had, as Dante said of his own work, paled his cheek. The Society he belonged to published a little magazine, and he had asked the readers to decide whether they preferred his prose or his verse, and it was because they so willed it that he wrote the little transcendental verses afterwards published in Homeward Songs by the Way.

Life was not expensive in that house, where, I think, no meat was eaten; I know that out of the sixty or seventy pounds a year which he earned as accountant in a Dublin shop, he saved a considerable portion for his private charity; and it was, I think, his benevolence that gave him his lucidity of speech, and, perhaps, of writing. If he convinced himself that any particular activity was desirable in the public interest or in that of his friends, he had at once the ardour that came to another from personal ambition. He was always surrounded with a little group of infirm or unlucky persons, whom he explained to themselves and to others, turning cat to griffin, goose to swan. In later years he was to accept the position of organizer of a co-operative banking system, before he had even read a book upon economics or finance, and within a few months to give evidence before a Royal Commission upon the system, as an acknowledged expert, though he had brought to it nothing but his impassioned versatility.

At the time I write of him, he was the religious teacher, and that alone, his painting, his poetry, and his conversation all subservient to that one end. Men watched him with awe or with bewilderment; it was known that he saw visions continually, perhaps more continually than any modern man since Swedenborg; and when he painted and drew in pastel what he had seen, some accepted the record without hesitation, others, like myself, noticing the academic Graeco-Roman forms, and remembering his early admiration for the works of Gustave Moreau, divined a subjective element, but no one doubted his word. One might not think him a good observer, but no one could doubt that he reported with the most scrupulous care what he believed himself to have seen; nor did he lack occasional objective corroboration. Walking with some man in his park, his demesne, as we say in Ireland, he had seen a visionary church at a particular spot, and the man had dug and uncovered its foundations; then some woman had met him with, "Oh, Mr Russell, I am so unhappy," and he had replied, "You will be perfectly happy this evening at seven o'clock," and left her to her blushes. She had an appointment with a young man for seven o'clock. I had heard of this a day or so after the event, and I asked him about it, and was told it had suddenly come into his head to use those words; but why he did not know. He and I often quarrelled, because I wanted him to examine and question his visions, and write them out as they occurred; and still more because I thought symbolic what he thought real like the men and women that had passed him on the road. Were they so much a part of his sub-conscious life that they would have vanished had he submitted them to question; were they like those voices that only speak, those strange sights that only show themselves for an instant, when the attention has been withdrawn; that phantasmagoria of which I had learnt something in London: and had his verse and his painting a like origin? And was that why the same hand that painted a certain dreamy, lovely sandy shore, now in the Dublin Municipal Gallery, could with great rapidity fill many canvases with poetical commonplace; and why, after writing Homeward Songs by the Way, where all is skilful and much exquisite, he would never again write a perfect book? Was it precisely because in Swedenborg alone the conscious and the sub-conscious became one, as in that marriage of the angels, which he has described as a contact of the whole being, that Coleridge thought Swedenborg both man and woman?

Russell's influence, which was already great, had more to support it than his versatility, or the mystery that surrounded him, for his sense of justice, and the daring that came from his own confidence in it, had made him the general counsellor. He would give endless time to a case of conscience, and no situation was too difficult for his clarity; and certainly some of the situations were difficult. I remember his being summoned to decide between two ladies who had quarrelled about a vacillating admirer, and called each other, to each other's faces, the worst names in our somewhat anaemic modern vocabulary; and I have heard of his success on an occasion when I think no other but Dostoievsky's idiot could have avoided offence. The Society was very young, and, as its members faced the world's moral complexities as though they were the first that ever faced them, they drew up very vigorous rules. One rule was that if any member saw a fault growing upon any other member, it was his duty to point it out to that member. A certain young man become convinced that a certain young woman had fallen in love with him; and, as an unwritten rule pronounced love and the spiritual life incompatible, that was a heavy fault. As the young man felt the delicacy of the situation, he asked for Russell's help, and side by side they braved the offender, who, I was told, received their admonishment with surprised humility, and promised amendment. His voice would often become high, and lose its self-possession during intimate conversation, and I especially could put him in a rage; but the moment the audience became too large for intimacy, or some exciting event had given formality to speech, he would be at the same moment impassioned and impersonal. He had, and has, the capacity, beyond that of any man I have known, to put with entire justice not only the thoughts, but the emotions, of the most opposite parties and personalities, as it were dissolving some public or private uproar into drama by Corneille or by Racine; and men who have hated each other must sometimes have been reconciled, because each heard his enemy's argument put into better words than he himself had found for his own; and this gift was in later years to give him political influence, and win him respect from Irish Nationalist and Unionist alike. It was, perhaps, because of it, joined to a too literal acceptance of those noble images of moral tradition which are so like late Graeco-Roman statues, that he had seen all human life as a mythological system, where, though all cats are griffins, the more dangerous griffins are only found among politicians he has not spoken to, or among authors he has but glanced at; while those men and women who bring him their confessions and listen to his advice, carry but the snowiest of swan's plumage. Nor has it failed to make him, as I think, a bad literary critic; demanding plays and poems where the characters must attain a stature of seven feet, and resenting as something perverse and morbid all abatement from that measure. I sometimes wonder what he would have been had he not met in early life the poetry of Emerson and Walt Whitman, writers who have begun to seem superficial precisely because they lack the Vision of evil; and those translations of the Upanishads, which it is so much harder to study by the sinking flame of Indian tradition than by the serviceable lamp of Emerson and Walt Whitman.

We are never satisfied with the maturity of those whom we have admired in boyhood; and, because we have seen their whole circle, even the most successful life is but a segment, we remain to the end their harshest critics. One old schoolfellow of mine will never believe that I have fulfilled the promise of some rough unscannable verses that I wrote before I was eighteen. Does any imaginative man find in maturity the admiration that his first half-articulate years aroused in some little circle; and is not the first success the greatest? Certainly, I demanded of Russell some impossible things, and if I had any influence upon him, and I have little doubt that I had, for we were very intimate, it may not have been a good influence for I thought there could be no aim for poet or artist except expression of a "Unity of Being" like that of a "perfectly proportioned human body", though I would not at the time have used that phrase. I remember that I was ironic and indignant when he left the Art Schools because his "will was weak, and must grow weaker if he followed any emotional pursuit;" as, later, when he let the readers of a magazine decide between his prose and his verse. I now know that there are men who cannot possess "Unity of Being," who must not seek it or express it, and who, so far from seeking an anti-self, a Mask that delineates a being in all things the opposite to their natural state, can but seek the suppression of the anti-self, till the natural state alone remains. These are those who must seek no image of desire, but await that which lies beyond their mind, unities not of the mind, but unities of nature, unities of God: the man of science, the moralist, the humanitarian, the politician, St. Simon Stylites upon his pillar, St. Antony in his cavern; all whose pre-occupation is to know themselves for fragments, and at last for nothing; to hollow their hearts out till they are void and without form, to summon a creator by revealing chaos, to become the lamp for another's wick and oil; and indeed it may be that it has been for their guidance in a very special sense that the "perfectly proportioned human body" suffered crucifixion. For them Mask and Image are of necessity morbid, turning their eyes upon themselves, as though they were of those who can be law unto themselves, of whom Chapman has written, "Neither is it lawful that they should stoop to any other law," whereas they are indeed of those who can but ask, "Have I behaved as well as So-and-so?" "Am I a good man according to the commandments?" or, "Do I realise my own nothingness before God?" "Have my experiments and observations excluded the personal factor with sufficient rigour?" Such men do not assume wisdom or beauty as Shelley did, when he masked himself as Ahasuerus, or as Prince Athanais, nor do they pursue an Image through a world that had else seemed an uninhabitable wilderness till, amid the privations of that pursuit, the Image is no more named Pandemos, but Urania; for such men must cast all Masks away and fly the Image, till that Image, transfigured because of their cruelties of self-abasement, becomes itself some Image or epitome of the whole natural or supernatural world, and itself pursues. The wholeness of the supernatural world can only express itself in personal form, because it has no epitome but man, nor can The Hound of Heaven fling itself into any but an empty heart. We may know the fugitives from others poets because, like George Herbert, like Francis Thompson, like George Russell, their imaginations grow more vivid in the expression of something which they have not themselves created, some historical religion or cause. But if the fugitive should live, as I think Russell does at times, as it is natural for a Morris or a Henley or a Shelley to live, hunters and pursuers all, his art surrenders itself to moral or poetical commonplace, to a repetition of thoughts and images that have no relation to experience.

I think that Russell would not have disappointed even my hopes had he, instead of meeting as an impressionable youth with our modern subjective romanticism, met with some form of traditional belief, which condemned all that romanticism admires and praises, indeed, all images of desire; for such condemnation would have turned his intellect towards the images of his vision. It might, doubtless, have embittered his life, for his strong intellect would have been driven out into the impersonal deeps where the man shudders; but it would have kept him a religious teacher, and set him, it may be, among the greatest of that species; politics, for a vision-seeking man, can be but half achievement, a choice of an almost easy kind of skill instead of that kind which is, of all those not impossible, the most difficult. Is it not certain that the Creator yawns in earthquake and thunder and other popular displays, but toils in rounding the delicate spiral of a shell?

XV

I heard the other day of a Dublin man recognizing in London an elderly man who had lived in that house in Ely Place in his youth, and of that elderly man, at the sudden memory, bursting into tears. Though I have no such poignant memories, for I was never of it, never anything but a dissatisfied critic, yet certain vivid moments come back to me as I write.

...Russell has just come in from a long walk on the Two Rock mountain, very full of his conversation with an old religious beggar, who kept repeating, "God possesses the heavens, but He covets the earth, He covets the earth."

I get in talk with a young man who has taken the orthodox side in some debate. He is a stranger, but explains that he has inherited magical art from his father, and asks me to his rooms to see it in operation. He and a friend of his kill a black cock, and burn herbs in a big bowl, but nothing happens except that the friend repeats again and again, "Oh, my God," and when I ask him why he has said that, does not know that he has spoken; and I feel that there is something very evil in the room.

We are sitting round the fire one night, and a member, a woman, tells a dream that she has just had. She dreamed that she saw monks digging in a garden. They dug down till they found a coffin, and when they took off the lid she saw that in the coffin lay a beautiful young man in a dress of gold brocade. The young man railed against the glory of the world, and when he had finished, the monks closed the coffin reverently, and buried it once more. They smoothed the ground, and then went on with their gardening.

I have a young man with me, an official of the National Literary Society, and I leave him in the reading-room with Russell, while I go upstairs to see the young Scotchman. I return after some minutes to find that the young man has become a Theosophist, but a month later, after an interview with a friar, to whom he gives an incredible account of his new beliefs, he goes to Mass again.

BOOK III

HODOS CAMELIONIS

I

When staying with Hyde in Roscommon, I had driven over to Lough Kay, hoping to find some local memory of the old story of Tumaus Costello, which I was turning into a story now called Proud Costello, Macdermot's Daughter, and the Bitter Tongue. I was rowed up the lake that I might find the island where he died; I had to find it from Hyde's account in The Love-Songs of Connaught, for when I asked the boatman, he told the story of Hero and Leander, putting Hero's house on one island, and Leander's on another. Presently we stopped to eat our sandwiches at the "Castle Rock," an island all castle. It was not an old castle, being but the invention of some romantic man, seventy or eighty years ago. The last man who had lived there had been Dr. Hyde's father, and he had but stayed a fortnight. The Gaelic-speaking men in the district were accustomed, instead of calling some specially useless thing a "white elephant," to call it "The Castle on the Rock." The roof was, however, still sound, and the windows unbroken. The situation in the centre of the lake, that has little wood-grown islands, and is surrounded by wood-grown hills, is romantic, and at one end, and perhaps at the other too, there is a stone platform where meditative persons might pace to and fro. I planned a mystical Order which should buy or hire the castle, and keep it as a place where its members could retire for a while for contemplation, and where we might establish mysteries like those of Eleusis and Samothrace; and for ten years to come my most impassioned thought was a vain attempt to find philosophy and to create ritual for that Order. I had an unshakeable conviction, arising how or whence I cannot tell, that invisible gates would open as they opened for Blake, as they opened for Swedenborg, as they opened for Boehme, and that this philosophy would find its manuals of devotion in all imaginative literature, and set before Irishmen for special manual an Irish literature which, though made by many minds, would seem the work of a single mind, and turn our places of beauty or legendary association into holy symbols. I did not think this philosophy would be altogether pagan, for it was plain that its symbols must be selected from all those things that had moved men most during many, mainly Christian, centuries.

I thought that for a time I could rhyme of love, calling it The Rose, because of the Rose's double meaning; of a fisherman who had "never a crack" in his heart; of an old woman complaining of the idleness of the young, or of some cheerful fiddler, all those things that "popular poets" write of, but that I must some day, on that day when the gates began to open, become difficult or obscure. With a rhythm that still echoed Morris I prayed to the Red Rose, to Intellectual Beauty:

"Come near, come near, come near, ah, leave me still   A little space for the Rose-breath to fill, Lest I no more hear common things.... But seek alone to hear the strange things said   By God to the bright hearts of those long dead,   And learn to chant a tongue men do not know."

I do not remember what I meant by "the bright hearts," but a little later I wrote of Spirits "with mirrors in their hearts."

My rituals were not to be made deliberately, like a poem, but all got by that method Mathers had explained to me, and with this hope I plunged without a clue into a labyrinth of images, into that labyrinth that we are warned against in those Oracles which antiquity has attributed to Zoroaster, but modern scholarship to some Alexandrian poet. "Stoop not down to the darkly splendid world wherein lieth continually a faithless depth and Hades wrapped in cloud, delighting in unintelligible images."

II

I found a supporter at Sligo in my elderly uncle, a man of fifty-three or fifty-four, with the habits of a much older man. He had never left the West of Ireland, except for a few days to London every year, and a single fortnight's voyage to Spain on board a trading schooner, in his boyhood. He was in politics a Unionist and Tory of the most obstinate kind, and knew nothing of Irish literature or history. He was, however, strangely beset by the romance of Ireland, as he discovered it among the people who served him, sailing upon his ships or attending to his horses, and, though narrow and obstinate of opinion, and puritanical in his judgment of life, was perhaps the most tolerant man I have ever known. He never expected anybody to agree with him, and if you did not upset his habits by cheating him over a horse, or by offending his taste, he would think as well of you as he did of other men, and that was not very well; and help you out of any scrape whatever. I was accustomed to people much better read than he, much more liberal-minded, but they had no life but the intellectual life, and if they and I differed, they could not take it lightly, and were often angry, and so for years now I had gone to Sligo, sometimes because I could not afford my Dublin lodging, but most often for freedom and peace. He would receive me with "I have learned that your friend So and So has been seen at the Gresham Hotel talking to Mr William Redmond. What will not people do for notoriety?" He considered all Irish Nationalist Members of Parliament as outside the social pale, but after dinner, when conversation grew intimate, would talk sympathetically of the Fenians in Ballina, where he spent his early manhood, or of the Fenian privateer that landed the wounded man at Sligo in the 'sixties. When Parnell was contesting an election at Sligo a little before his death, other Unionist magistrates refused or made difficulties when asked for some assistance, what I do not remember, made necessary under election law; and so my uncle gave that assistance. He walked up and down some Town Hall assembly-room or some courtroom with Parnell, but would tell me nothing of that conversation, except that Parnell spoke of Gladstone with extravagant hatred. He would not repeat words spoken by a great man in his bitterness, yet Parnell at the moment was too angry to care who listened. I knew one other man who kept as firm a silence; he had attended Parnell's last public meeting, and after it sat alone beside him, and heard him speak of the followers that had fallen away, or were showing their faint hearts; but Parnell was the chief devotion of his life.

When I first began my visits, he had lived in the town itself, and close to a disreputable neighbourhood called the Burrough, till one evening, while he sat over his dinner, he heard a man and woman quarrelling under his window. "I mind the time," shouted the man, "when I slept with you and your daughter in the one bed." My uncle was horrified, and moved to a little house about a quarter of a mile into the country, where he lived with an old second-sighted servant, and a man-servant to look after the racehorse that was browsing in the neighbouring field, with a donkey to keep it company. His furniture had not been changed since he set up house for himself as a very young man, and in a room opposite his dining-room were the saddles of his youth, and though he would soon give up riding, they would be oiled and the stirrups kept clean and bright till the day of his death. Some love-affair had gone wrong when he was a very young man; he had now no interest in women; certainly never sought favour of a woman, and yet he took great care of his appearance. He did not let his beard grow, though he had, or believed that he had, for he was hypochondriacal, a sensitiveness of the skin that forced him to spend an hour in shaving, and he would take to club and dumb-bell if his waist thickened by a hair's breadth, and twenty years after, when a very old man, he had the erect shapely figure of his youth. I often wondered why he went through so much labour, for it was not pride, which had seemed histrionic in his eyes, and certainly he had no vanity; and now, looking back, I am convinced that it was from habit, mere habit, a habit formed when he was a young man, and the best rider of his district.

Probably through long association with Mary Battle, the second-sighted servant, he had come to believe much in the supernatural world, and would tell how several times, arriving home with an unexpected guest, he had found the table set for three, and that he himself had dreamed of his brother's illness in Liverpool before he had other news of it. He saw me using images learned from Mathers to start reverie, and, though I held out for a long time, thinking him too old and habit-bound, he persuaded me to tell him their use, and from that on we experimented continually, and after a time I began to keep careful record. In summer he always had the same little house at Rosses Point, and it was there that he first became sensitive to the cabalistic symbols. There are some high sandhills and low cliffs, and I adopted the practice of walking by the seashore while he walked on cliff or sandhill; I, without speaking, would imagine the symbol, and he would notice what passed before his mind's eye, and in a short time he would practically never fail of the appropriate vision. In the symbols which are used certain colours are classified as "actives," while certain other colours are "passives," and I had soon discovered that if I used "actives" George Pollexfen would see nothing. I therefore gave him exercises to make him sensitive to those colours, and gradually we found ourselves well fitted for this work, and he began to take as lively an interest, as was possible to a nature given over to habit, in my plans for the Castle on the Rock.

I worked with others, sworn to the scheme for the most part, and I made many curious observations. It was the symbol itself, or, at any rate, not my conscious intention that produced the effect, for if I made an error and told someone, let us say, to gaze at the wrong symbol, they were painted upon cards, the vision would be suggested by the symbol, not by my thought, or two visions would appear side by side, one from the symbol and one from my thought. When two people, between whose minds there was even a casual sympathy, worked together under the same symbolic influence, the dream or reverie would divide itself between them, each half being the complement of the other; and now and again these complementary dreams, or reveries, would arise spontaneously. I find, for instance, in an old notebook, "I saw quite suddenly a tent with a wooden badly-carved idol, painted dull red; a man looking like a Red Indian was prostrate before it. The idol was seated to the left. I asked G. what he saw. He saw a most august immense being, glowing with a ruddy opalescent colour, sitting on a throne to the left", or, to summarise from a later notebook,... I am meditating in one room and my fellow-student in another, when I see a boat full of tumult and movement on a still sea, and my friend sees a boat with motionless sails upon a tumultuous sea. There was nothing in the originating symbol to suggest a boat.

We never began our work until George's old servant was in her bed; and yet, when we went upstairs to our beds, we constantly heard her crying out with nightmare, and in the morning we would find that her dream echoed our vision. One night, started by what symbol I forget, we had seen an allegorical marriage of Heaven and Earth. When Mary Battle brought in the breakfast next morning, I said, "Well, Mary, did you dream anything last night?" and she replied (I am quoting from an old notebook) "indeed she had," and that it was "a dream she would not have liked to have had twice in one night." She had dreamed that her bishop, the Catholic bishop of Sligo, had gone away "without telling anybody," and had married "a very high-up lady," "and she not too young, either." She had thought in her dream, "Now all the clergy will get married, and it will be no use going to confession." There were "layers upon layers of flowers, many roses, all round the church."

Another time, when George Pollexfen had seen in answer to some evocation of mine a man with his head cut in two, she woke to find that she "must have cut her face with a pin, as it was all over blood." When three or four saw together, the dream or vision would divide itself into three or four parts, each seeming complete in itself, and all fitting together, so that each part was an adaptation of a single meaning to a particular personality. A visionary being would give, let us say, a lighted torch to one, an unlighted candle to another, an unripe fruit to a third, and to the fourth a ripe fruit. At times coherent stories were built up, as if a company of actors were to improvise, and play, not only without previous consultation, but without foreseeing at any moment what would be said or done the moment after. Who made the story? Was it the mind of one of the visionaries? Perhaps, for I have endless proof that, where two worked together, the symbolic influence commonly took upon itself, though no word was spoken, the quality of the mind that had first fixed a symbol in the mind's eye. But, if so, what part of the mind? One friend, in whom the symbolic impulse produced actual trance, described an elaborate and very strange story while the trance was upon him, but upon waking told a story that after a certain point was quite different. "They gave me a cup of wine, and after that I remembered nothing." While speaking out of trance he had said nothing of the cup of wine, which must have been offered to a portion of his mind quite early in the dream. Then, too, from whence come the images of the dream? Not always, I was soon persuaded, from the memory, perhaps never in trance or sleep. One man, who certainly thought that Eve's apple was the sort that you got from the greengrocer, and as certainly never doubted its story's literal truth, said, when I used some symbol to send him to Eden, that he saw a walled garden on the top of a high mountain, and in the middle of it a tree with great birds in the branches, and fruit out of which, if you held a fruit to your ear, came the sound of fighting. I had not at the time read Dante's Purgatorio, and it caused me some trouble to verify the mountain garden, and, from some passage in the Zohar, the great birds among the boughs; while a young girl, on being sent to the same garden, heard "the music of heaven" from a tree, and on listening with her ear against the trunk, found that it was made by the "continual clashing of swords." Whence came that fine thought of music-making swords, that image of the garden, and many like images and thoughts? I had as yet no clear answer, but knew myself face to face with the Anima Mundi described by Platonic philosophers, and more especially in modern times by Henry More, which has a memory independent of individual memories, though they constantly enrich it with their images and their thoughts.

III

At Sligo we walked twice every day, once after lunch and once after dinner, to the same gate on the road to Knocknarea; and at Rosses Point, to the same rock upon the shore; and as we walked we exchanged those thoughts that never rise before me now without bringing some sight of mountain or of shore. Considering that Mary Battle received our thoughts in sleep, though coarsened or turned to caricature, do not the thoughts of the scholar or the hermit, though they speak no word, or something of their shape and impulse, pass into the general mind? Does not the emotion of some woman of fashion, caught in the subtle torture of self-analysing passion, pass down, although she speak no word, to Joan with her Pot, Jill with her Pail and, it may be, with one knows not what nightmare melancholy to Tom the Fool?

Seeing that a vision could divide itself in divers complementary portions, might not the thought of philosopher or poet or mathematician depend at every moment of its progress upon some complementary thought in minds perhaps at a great distance? Is there nation-wide multiform reverie, every mind passing through a stream of suggestion, and all streams acting and reacting upon one another, no matter how distant the minds, how dumb the lips? A man walked, as it were, casting a shadow, and yet one could never say which was man and which was shadow, or how many the shadows that he cast. Was not a nation, as distinguished from a crowd of chance comers, bound together by these parallel streams or shadows; that Unity of Image, which I sought in national literature, being but an originating symbol?

From the moment when these speculations grew vivid, I had created for myself an intellectual solitude, most arguments that could influence action had lost something of their meaning. How could I judge any scheme of education, or of social reform, when I could not measure what the different classes and occupations contributed to that invisible commerce of reverie and of sleep; and what is luxury and what necessity when a fragment of gold braid, or a flower in the wallpaper may be an originating impulse to revolution or to philosophy? I began to feel myself not only solitary but helpless.

IV

I had not taken up these subjects wilfully, nor through love of strangeness, nor love of excitement, nor because I found myself in some experimental circle, but because unaccountable things had happened even in my childhood, and because of an ungovernable craving. When supernatural events begin, a man first doubts his own testimony, but when they repeat themselves again and again, he doubts all human testimony. At least he knows his own bias, and may perhaps allow for it, but how trust historian and psychologist that have for two hundred years ignored in writing of the history of the world, or of the human mind, so momentous a part of human experience? What else had they ignored and distorted? When Mesmerists first travelled about as public entertainers, a favourite trick was to tell a mesmerised man that some letter of the alphabet had ceased to exist, and after that to make him write his name upon the blackboard. Brown, or Jones, or Robinson would become upon the instant, and without any surprise or hesitation, Rown, or Ones, or Obinson.

Was modern civilisation a conspiracy of the sub-conscious? Did we turn away from certain thoughts and things because the Middle Ages lived in terror of the dark, or had some seminal illusion been imposed upon us by beings greater than ourselves for an unknown purpose? Even when no facts of experience were denied, might not what had seemed logical proof be but a mechanism of change, an automatic impulse? Once in London, at a dinner party, where all the guests were intimate friends, I had written upon a piece of paper, "In five minutes York Powell will talk of a burning house," thrust the paper under my neighbour's plate, and imagined my fire symbol, and waited in silence. Powell shifted conversation from topic to topic and within the five minutes was describing a fire he had seen as a young man. When Locke's French translator Coste asked him how, if there were no "innate ideas," he could explain the skill shown by a bird in making its nest, Locke replied, "I did not write to explain the actions of dumb creatures," and his translator thought the answer "very good, seeing that he had named his book A Philosophical Essay upon Human Understanding." Henry More, upon the other hand, considered that the bird's instinct proved the existence of the Anima Mundi, with its ideas and memories. Did modern enlightenment think with Coste that Locke had the better logic, because it was not free to think otherwise?

V

I ceased to read modern books that were not books of belief older than any European Church, and founded that interested me, I tried to trace it back to its earliest use, believing that there must be a tradition of belief older than any European Church, and founded upon the experience of the world before the modern bias. It was this search for a tradition that urged George Pollexfen and myself to study the visions and thoughts of the country people, and some country conversation repeated by one or the other often gave us a day's discussion. These visions, we soon discovered, were very like those we called up by symbol. Mary Battle, looking out of the window at Rosses Point, saw coming from Knocknarea, where Queen Maeve, according to local folklore, is buried under a great heap of stones, "the finest woman you ever saw travelling right across from the mountains and straight to here." I quote a record written at the time. "She looked very strong, but not wicked" (that is to say, not cruel). "I have seen the Irish Giant" (some big man shown at a fair). "And though he was a fine man he was nothing to her, for he was round and could not have stepped out so soldierly ... she had no stomach on her but was slight and broad in the shoulders, and was handsomer than any one you ever saw; she looked about thirty." And when I asked if she had seen others like her, she said, "Some of them have their hair down, but they look quite different, more like the sleepy-looking ladies one sees in the papers. Those with their hair up are like this one. The others have long white dresses, but those with their hair up have short dresses, so that you can see their legs right up to the calf." And when I questioned her, I found that they wore what might well be some kind of buskin. "They are fine and dashing-looking, like the men one sees riding their horses in twos and threes on the slopes of the mountains with their swords swinging. There is no such race living now, none so finely proportioned ... When I think of her and the ladies now they are like little children running about not knowing how to put their clothes on right ... why, I would not call them women at all."

Not at this time, but some three or four years later, when the visions came without any conscious use of symbol for a short time, and with much greater vividness, I saw two or three forms of this incredible beauty, one especially that must always haunt my memory. Then, too, the Master Pilot told us of meeting at night close to the Pilot House a procession of women in what seemed the costume of another age. Were they really people of the past, revisiting, perhaps, the places where they lived, or must I explain them, as I explained that vision of Eden as a mountain garden, by some memory of the race, as distinct from individual memory? Certainly these Spirits, as the country people called them, seemed full of personality; were they not capricious, generous, spiteful, anxious, angry, and yet did that prove them more than images and symbols? When I used a combined earth and fire and lunar symbol, my seer, a girl of twenty-five, saw an obvious Diana and her dogs, about a fire in a cavern. Presently, judging from her closed eyes, and from the tone of her voice, that she was in trance, not in reverie, I wished to lighten the trance a little, and made through carelessness or hasty thinking a symbol of dismissal; and at once she started and cried out, "She says you are driving her away too quickly. You have made her angry." Then, too, if my visions had a subjective element, so had Mary Battle's, for her fairies had but one tune, The Distant Waterfall, and she never heard anything described in a sermon at the Cathedral that she did not "see it after," and spoke of seeing in this way the gates of Purgatory.

Furthermore, if my images could affect her dreams, the folk-images could affect mine in turn, for one night I saw between sleeping and waking a strange long bodied pair of dogs, one black and one white, that I found presently in some country tale. How, too, could one separate the dogs of the country tale from those my uncle heard bay in his pillow? In order to keep myself from nightmare, I had formed the habit of imagining four watch-dogs, one at each corner of my room, and, though I had not told him or anybody, he said, "Here is a very curious thing; most nights now, when I lay my head upon the pillow, I hear a sound of dogs baying, the sound seems to come up out of the pillow." A friend of Strindberg's, in delirium tremens, was haunted by mice, and a friend in the next room heard the squealing of the mice.

VI

To that multiplicity of interest and opinion, of arts and sciences, which had driven me to conceive a Unity of Culture defined and evoked by Unity of Image, I had but added a multiplicity of images, and I was the more troubled because, the first excitement over, I had done nothing to rouse George Pollexfen from the gloom and hypochondria always thickening about him. I asked no help of books, for I believed that the truth I sought would come to me like the subject of a poem, from some moment of passionate experience, and that if I filled my exposition with other men's thought, other men's investigation, I would sink into all that multiplicity of interest and opinion. That passionate experience could never come, of that I was certain, until I had found the right image or right images. From what but the image of Apollo, fixed always in memory and passion, did his priesthood get that occasional power, a classical historian has described, of lifting great stones and snapping great branches; and did not Gemma Galgani, like many others that had gone before, in 1889 cause deep wounds to appear in her body by contemplating her crucifix? In the essay that Wilde read to me one Christmas Day, occurred these words, "What does not the world owe to the imitation of Christ, what to the imitation of Caesar?" and I had seen Macgregor Mathers paint little pictures combining the forms of men, animals, and birds, according to a rule which provided a form for every possible mental condition, and I had heard him describing, upon what authority I do not remember, how citizens of ancient Egypt assumed, when in contemplation, the images of their gods.

But now image called up image in an endless procession, and I could not always choose among them with any confidence; and when I did choose, the image lost its intensity, or changed into some other image. I had but exchanged the Temptation of Flaubert's Bouvard et Pecuchet for that of his St. Anthony, and I was lost in that region a cabalistic manuscript, shown me by Macgregor Mathers, had warned me of; astray upon the Path of the Cameleon, upon Hodos Camelionis.

VII

Now that I am a settled man and have many birds, the canaries have just hatched out four nestlings, I have before me the problem that Locke waved aside. As I gave them an artificial nest, a hollow vessel like a saucer, they had no need of that skill the wild bird shows, each species having its own preference among the lichen, or moss; but they could sort out wool and hair and a certain soft white down that I found under a big tree. They would twist a stem of grass till it was limber, and would wind it all about the centre of the nest, and when the four grey eggs were laid, the mother bird knew how to turn them over from time to time, that they might be warmed evenly; and how long she must leave them uncovered, that the white might not be dried up, and when to return that the growing bird might not take cold. Then the young birds, even when they had all their feathers, were very still as compared with the older birds, as though any habit of movement would disturb the nest or make them tumble out. One of them would now and again pass on the food that he had received from his mother's beak to some other nestling. The father had often pecked the mother bird before the eggs were laid, but now, until the last nestling was decently feathered, he took his share in the feeding, and was very peaceable, and it was only when the young could be left to feed themselves that he grew jealous and had to be put into another cage.

When I watch my child, who is not yet three years old, I can see so many signs of knowledge from beyond her own mind; why else should she be so excited when a little boy passes outside the window, and take so little interest in a girl; why should she put a cloak about her, and look over her shoulder to see it trailing upon the stairs, as she will someday trail a dress; and why, above all, as she lay against her mother's side, and felt the unborn child moving within, did she murmur, "Baby, baby?"

When a man writes any work of genius, or invents some creative action, is it not because some knowledge or power has come into his mind from beyond his mind? It is called up by an image, as I think; all my birds' adventures started when I hung a little saucer at one side of the cage, and at the other a bundle of hair and grass; but our images must be given to us, we cannot choose them deliberately.

VIII

I know now that revelation is from the self, but from that age-long memoried self, that shapes the elaborate shell of the mollusc and the child in the womb, that teaches the birds to make their nest; and that genius is a crisis that joins that buried self for certain moments to our trivial daily mind. There are, indeed, personifying spirits that we had best call but Gates and Gate-keepers, because through their dramatic power they bring our souls to crisis, to Mask and Image, caring not a straw whether we be Juliet going to her wedding, or Cleopatra to her death; for in their eyes nothing has weight but passion. We have dreamed a foolish dream these many centuries in thinking that they value a life of contemplation, for they scorn that more than any possible life, unless it be but a name for the worst crisis of all. They have but one purpose, to bring their chosen man to the greatest obstacle he may confront without despair. They contrived Dante's banishment, and snatched away his Beatrice, and thrust Villon into the arms of harlots, and sent him to gather cronies at the foot of the gallows, that Dante and Villon might through passion become conjoint to their buried selves, turn all to Mask and Image, and so be phantoms in their own eyes. In great lesser writers like Landor and like Keats we are shown that Image and that Mask as something set apart; Andromeda and her Perseus, though not the sea-dragon, but in a few in whom we recognise supreme masters of tragedy, the whole contest is brought into the circle of their beauty. Such masters, Villon and Dante, let us say, would not, when they speak through their art, change their luck; yet they are mirrored in all the suffering of desire. The two halves of their nature are so completely joined that they seem to labour for their objects, and yet to desire whatever happens, being at the same instant predestinate and free, creation's very self. We gaze at such men in awe, because we gaze not at a work of art, but at the re-creation of the man through that art, the birth of a new species of man, and, it may even seem that the hairs of our heads stand up, because that birth, that re-creation, is from terror. Had not Dante and Villon understood that their fate wrecked what life could not rebuild, had they lacked their Vision of Evil, had they cherished any species of optimism, they could but have found a false beauty, or some momentary instinctive beauty, and suffered no change at all, or but changed as do the wild creatures, or from devil well to devil sick, and so round the clock.

They and their sort alone earn contemplation, for it is only when the intellect has wrought the whole of life to drama, to crisis, that we may live for contemplation, and yet keep our intensity.

And these things are true also of nations, but the Gate-keepers who drive the nation to war or anarchy that it may find its Image are different from those who drive individual men, though I think at times they work together. And as I look backward upon my own writing, I take pleasure alone in those verses where it seems to me I have found something hard, cold, some articulation of the Image, which is the opposite of all that I am in my daily life, and all that my country is; yet man or nation can no more make Mask or Image than the seed can be made by the soil into which it is cast.

Ille.

"What portion in the world can the artist have,
Who has awakened from the common dream,
But dissipation and despair?

Hic.

And yet
No one denies to Keats, love of the world.
Remember his deliberate happiness.

Ille.

His art is happy, but who knows his mind?
I see a schoolboy, when I think of him,
With face and nose pressed to a sweet-shop window.
For certainly he sank into his grave
His senses and his heart unsatisfied,
And made, being poor, ailing, and ignorant....
Shut out from all the luxury of the world,
Luxuriant song."

BOOK IV

THE TRAGIC GENERATION

Two or three years after our return to Bedford Park The Doll's House had been played at the Royalty Theatre in Dean Street, the first Ibsen play to be played in England, and somebody had given me a seat for the gallery. In the middle of the first act, while the heroine was asking for macaroons, a middle-aged washerwoman who sat in front of me, stood up and said to the little boy at her side, "Tommy, if you promise to go home straight, we will go now;" and at the end of the play, as I wandered through the entrance hall, I heard an elderly critic murmur, "A series of conversations terminated by an accident." I was divided in mind, I hated the play; what was it but Carolus Durand, Bastien-Lepage, Huxley and Tyndall, all over again; I resented being invited to admire dialogue so close to modern educated speech that music and style were impossible.

"Art is art because it is not nature," I kept repeating to myself, but how could I take the same side with critic and washerwoman? As time passed Ibsen became in my eyes the chosen author of very clever young journalists, who, condemned to their treadmill of abstraction, hated music and style; and yet neither I nor my generation could escape him because, though we and he had not the same friends, we had the same enemies. I bought his collected works in Mr. Archer's translation out of my thirty shillings a week and carried them to and fro upon my journeys to Ireland and Sligo, and Florence Farr, who had but one great gift, the most perfect poetical elocution, became prominent as an Ibsen actress and had almost a success in Rosmersholm, where there is symbolism and a stale odour of spoilt poetry. She and I and half our friends found ourselves involved in a quarrel with the supporters of old fashioned melodrama, and conventional romance, and in the support of the new dramatists who wrote in what the Daily Press chose to consider the manner of Ibsen. In 1894 she became manageress of the Avenue Theatre with a play of Dr. Todhunter's, called The Comedy of Sighs, and Mr Bernard Shaw's Arms and the Man. She asked me to write a one act play for her niece, Miss Dorothy Paget, a girl of eight or nine, to make her first stage appearance in; and I, with my Irish Theatre in mind, wrote The Land of Heart's Desire, in some discomfort when the child was theme, as I knew nothing of children, but with an abundant mind when Mary Bruin was for I knew an Irish woman whose unrest troubled me and lay beyond my comprehension. When she opened her theatre she had to meet a hostile audience, almost as violent as that Synge met in January, 1907, and certainly more brutal, for the Abbey audience had no hatred for the players, and I think but little for Synge himself. Nor had she the certainty of final victory to give her courage, for The Comedy of Sighs was a rambling story told with a little paradoxical wit. She had brought the trouble upon herself perhaps, for always in revolt against her own poetical gift, which now seemed obsolete, and against her own Demeter-like face in the mirror, she had tried when interviewed by the Press to shock and startle, to seem to desire enemies; and yet, unsure of her own judgment being out of her own trade, had feared to begin with Shaw's athletic wit, and now outraged convention saw its chance. For two hours and a half, pit and gallery drowned the voices of the players with boos and jeers that were meant to be bitter to the author who sat visible to all in his box surrounded by his family, and to the actress struggling bravely through her weary part; and then pit and gallery went home to spread their lying story that the actress had a fit of hysterics in her dressing-room.

Todhunter had sat on to the end, and there were, I think, four acts of it, listening to the howling of his enemies, while his friends slipped out one by one, till one saw everywhere their empty seats, but nothing could arouse the fighting instincts of that melancholy man. Next day I tried to get him to publish his book of words with satirical designs and illustrations, by Beardsley, who was just rising into fame, and an introduction attacking the public, but though petulant and irascible he was incapable of any emotion that could give life to a cause. He shared the superstition still current in the theatre, that the public wants sincere drama, but is kept from it by some conspiracy of managers or newspapers, and could not get out of his head that the actors were to blame. Shaw, whose turn came next, had foreseen all months before, and had planned an opening that would confound his enemies. For the first few minutes Arms and the Man is crude melodrama and then just when the audience are thinking how crude it is, it turns into excellent farce. At the dress rehearsal, a dramatist who had his own quarrel with the public, was taken in the noose; for at the first laugh he stood up, turned his back on the stage, scowled at the audience, and even when everybody else knew what turn the play had taken, continued to scowl, and order those nearest to be silent.

On the first night the whole pit and gallery, except certain members of the Fabian Society, started to laugh at the author and then, discovering that they themselves were being laughed at, sat there not converted, their hatred was too bitter for that, but dumbfounded, while the rest of the house cheered and laughed. In the silence that greeted the author after the cry for a speech one man did indeed get his courage and boo loudly. "I assure the gentleman in the gallery," was Shaw's answer, "that he and I are of exactly the same opinion, but what can we do against a whole house who are of the contrary opinion?" And from that moment Bernard Shaw became the most formidable man in modern letters, and even the most drunken of medical students knew it. My own play, which had been played with The Comedy of Sighs, had roused no passions, but had pleased a sufficient minority for Florence Farr to keep it upon the stage with Arms and the Man, and I was in the theatre almost every night for some weeks. "Oh, yes, the people seem to like Arms and the Man," said one of Mr Shaw's players to me, "but we have just found out that we are all wrong. Mr Shaw did really mean it quite seriously, for he has written a letter to say so, and we must not play for laughs anymore." Another night I found the manager, triumphant and excited, the Prince of Wales and the Duke of Edinburgh had been there, and the Duke of Edinburgh had spoken his dislike out loud so that the whole stalls could hear, but the Prince of Wales had been "very pleasant" and "got the Duke of Edinburgh away as soon as possible." "They asked for me," he went on, "and the Duke of Edinburgh kept on repeating, 'The man is mad,' meaning Mr Shaw, and the Prince of Wales asked who Mr Shaw was, and what he meant by it." I myself was almost as bewildered for though I came mainly to see how my own play went, and for the first fortnight to vex my most patient actors with new lines, I listened with excitement to see how the audience would like certain passages of Arms and the Man. I hated it; it seemed to me inorganic, logical straightness and not the crooked road of life and I stood aghast before its energy as to-day before that of the Stone Drill by Mr. Epstein or of some design by Mr Wyndham Lewis. He was right to claim Samuel Butler for his master, for Butler was the first Englishman to make the discovery, that it is possible to write with great effect without music, without style, either good or bad, to eliminate from the mind all emotional implication and to prefer plain water to every vintage, so much metropolitan lead and solder to any tendril of the vine. Presently I had a nightmare that I was haunted by a sewing machine, that clicked and shone, but the incredible thing was that the machine smiled, smiled perpetually. Yet I delighted in Shaw the formidable man. He could hit my enemies and the enemies of all I loved, as I could never hit, as no living author that was dear to me could ever hit.

Florence Farr's way home was mine also for a part of the way, and it was often of this that we talked, and sometimes, though not always, she would share my hesitations, and for years to come I was to wonder whenever Shaw became my topic, whether the cock crowed for my blame or for my praise.

II

Shaw and Wilde, had no catastrophe come, would have long divided the stage between them, though they were most unlike, for Wilde believed himself to value nothing but words in their emotional associations, and he had turned his style to a parade as though it were his show, and he Lord Mayor.

I was at Sligo again and I saw the announcement of his action against Lord Queensberry, when starting from my uncle's house to walk to Knocknarea to dine with Cochrane of the Glen, as he was called, to distinguish him from others of that name, an able old man. He had a relation, a poor mad girl, who shared our meals, and at whom I shuddered. She would take a flower from the vase in front of her and push it along the tablecloth towards any male guest who sat near. The old man himself had strange opinions, born not from any mental eccentricity, but from the solitude of his life; and a freedom from all prejudice that was not of his own discovery. "The world is getting more manly," he would say, "it has begun to drink port again," or "Ireland is going to become prosperous. Divorced couples now choose Ireland for a retreat, just as before Scotland became prosperous they began to go there. There are a divorced wife and her lover living at the other side of the mountain." I remember that I spoke that night of Wilde's kindness to myself, said I did not believe him guilty, quoted the psychologist Bain, who has attributed to every sensualist "a voluminous tenderness," and described Wilde's hard brilliance, his dominating self-possession. I considered him essentially a man of action, that he was a writer by perversity and accident, and would have been more important as soldier or politician; and I was certain that, guilty or not guilty, he would prove himself a man. I was probably excited, and did most of the talking, for if Cochrane had talked, I would have remembered an amusing sentence or two; but he was certainly sympathetic. A couple of days later I received a letter from Lionel Johnson, denouncing Wilde with great bitterness. He had "a cold scientific intellect;" he got a "sense of triumph and power; at every dinner-table he dominated, from the knowledge that he was guilty of that sin which, more than any other possible to man, would turn all those people against him if they but knew." He wrote in the mood of his poem, To the Destroyer of a Soul, addressed to Wilde, as I have always believed, though I know nothing of the circumstance that made him write it.

I might have known that Wilde's phantasy had taken some tragic turn, and that he was meditating upon possible disaster, but one took all his words for play, had he not called insincerity "a mere multiplication of the personality" or some such words? I had met a man who had found him in a barber's shop in Venice, and heard him explain, "I am having my hair curled that I may resemble Nero;" and when, as editor of an Irish anthology, I had asked leave to quote "Tread gently, she is near under the snow," he had written that I might do so if I pleased, but his most characteristic poem was that sonnet with the lines

"Lo! with a little rod
I did but touch the honey's romance
And must I lose a soul's inheritance."

When in London for my play I had asked news from an actor who had seen him constantly. "He is in deep melancholy," was the answer. "He says that he tries to sleep away as much of life as possible, only leaving his bed at two or three in the afternoon, and spending the rest of the day at the Café Royal. He has written what he calls the best short story in the world, and will have it that he repeats to himself on getting out of bed and before every meal. 'Christ came from a white plain to a purple city, and as he passed through the first street, he heard voices overhead, and saw a young man lying drunk upon a window sill, "Why do you waste your soul in drunkenness?" He said. "Lord, I was a leper and You healed me, what else can I do?" A little further through the town he saw a young man following a harlot, and said, "Why do you dissolve your soul in debauchery?" and the young man answered, "Lord, I was blind, and You healed me, what else can I do?" At last in the middle of the city He saw an old man crouching, weeping upon the ground, and when He asked why he wept, the old man answered, "Lord, I was dead and You raised me into life, what else can I do but weep?"'"

Wilde published that story a little later, but spoiled it with the verbal decoration of his epoch, and I have to repeat it to myself as I first heard it, before I can see its terrible beauty. I no more doubt its sincerity than I doubt that his parade of gloom, all that late rising, and sleeping away his life, that elaborate playing with tragedy, was an attempt to escape from an emotion by its exaggeration. He had three successful plays running at once; he had been almost poor, and now, his head full of Flaubert, found himself with ten thousand a year: "Lord, I was dead, and You raised me into life, what else can I do but weep." A comedian, he was in the hands of those dramatists who understand nothing but tragedy.

A few days after the first production of my Land of Heart's Desire, I had my last conversation with him. He had come into the theatre as the curtain fell upon my play, and I knew that it was to ask my pardon that he overwhelmed me with compliments; and yet I wonder if he would have chosen those precise compliments, or spoken so extravagantly, but for the turn his thoughts had taken: "Your story in The National Observer, The Crucifixion of the Outcast, is sublime, wonderful, wonderful."

Some business or other brought me to London once more and I asked various Irish writers for letters of sympathy, and I was refused by none but Edward Dowden, who gave me what I considered an irrelevant excuse, his dislike for everything that Wilde had written. I heard that Wilde was at his mother's house in Oakley Street, and I called there, but the Irish servant told me, her face drawn and tragic as in the presence of death, that he was not there, but that I could see his brother. Willie Wilde received me with, "Who are you; what do you want?" but became all friendship when I told him that I had brought letters of sympathy. He took the bundle of letters in his hand, but said, "Do these letters urge him to run away? Every friend he has is urging him to, but we have made up our minds that he must stay and take his chance." "No," I said, "I certainly do not think that he should run away, nor do those letters advise it." "Letters from Ireland," he said. "Thank you, thank you. He will be glad to get those letters, but I would keep them from him if they advised him to run away." Then he threw himself back in his chair and began to talk with incoherent emotion, and in phrases that echoed now and again his brother's style at its worst; there were tear in his eyes, and he was, I think, slightly intoxicated. "He could escape, oh, yes, he could escape, there is a yacht in the Thames, and five thousand pounds to pay his bail, well, not exactly in the Thames, but there is a yacht, oh, yes, he could escape, even if I had to inflate a balloon in the back yard with my own hand, but he has resolved to stay, to face it out, to stand the music like Christ. You must have heard, it is not necessary to go into detail, but he and I, we have not been friends; but he came to me like a wounded stag, and I took him in." "After his release", after the failure of his action against Lord Queensberry, I think, "Stewart Headlam engaged a room at an hotel and brought him there under another name, but the manager came up and said, 'Are you Mr. Wilde?' You know what my brother is, you know how he would answer that. He said, 'Yes, I am Oscar Wilde,' and the manager said he must not stay. The same thing happened in hotel after hotel, and at last he made up his mind to come here. It is his vanity that has brought all this disgrace upon him; they swung incense before him." He dwelt upon the rhythm of the words as his brother would have done, "They swung it before his heart." His first emotion at the thought of the letters over, he became more simple, and explained that his brother considered that his crime was not the vice itself, but that he should have brought such misery upon his wife and children, and that he was bound to accept any chance, however slight, that might reestablish his position. "If he is acquitted," he said, "he will stay out of England for a few years, and can then gather his friends about him once more, even if he is condemned he will purge his offence, but if he runs away he will lose every friend that he has." I heard later, from whom I forget now, that Lady Wilde had said, "If you stay, even if you go to prison, you will always be my son, it will make no difference to my affection, but if you go, I will never speak to you again." While I was there, some woman who had just seen him, Willie Wilde's wife, I think, came in, and threw herself in a chair, and said in an exhausted voice, "It is all right now, he has made up his mind to go to prison if necessary." Before his release, two years later, his brother and mother were dead, and a little later his wife, struck by paralysis during his imprisonment, I think, was dead, too; and he himself, his constitution ruined by prison life, followed quickly; but I have never doubted, even for an instant, that he made the right decision, and that he owes to that decision half of his renown.

Cultivated London, that before the action against Lord Queensberry had mocked his pose and affected style, and refused to acknowledge his wit, was now full of his advocates, though I did not meet a single man who considered him innocent. One old enemy of his overtook me in the street and began to praise his audacity, his self-possession. "He has made," he said, "of infamy a new Thermopylae." I had written in reply to Lionel Johnson's letter that I regretted Wilde's downfall but not that of his imitators, but Johnson had changed with the rest. "Why do you not regret the fall of Wilde's imitators", I had but tried to share what I thought his opinion, "They were worthless, but should have been left to criticism." Wilde himself was a martyr in his eyes, and when I said that tragedy might give his art a greater depth, he would not even grant a martyr's enemies that poor merit, and thought Wilde would produce, when it was all over, some comedy exactly like the others, writing from an art where events could leave no trace. Everywhere one met writers and artists who praised his wit and eloquence in the witness box, or repeated some private saying. Willie Redmond told of finding him, to his astonishment, at the conversazione of some theatrical society, standing amid an infuriated crowd, mocking with more than all his old satirical wit the actors and their country. He had said to a well-known painter during one or other of the trials, "My poor brother writes to me that he is defending me all over London; my poor, dear brother, he could compromise a steam engine." His brother, too, had suffered a change, for, if rumour did not wrong him, "the wounded stag" had not been at all graciously received. "Thank God my vices were decent," had been his comment, and refusing to sit at the same table, he had dined at some neighbouring hotel at his brother's expense. His successful brother who had scorned him for a drunken ne'er-do-well was now at his mercy, and besides, he probably shared, until tragedy awoke another self, the rage and contempt that filled the crowds in the street, and all men and women who had an over-abundant normal sexual instinct. "Wilde will never lift his head again," said the art critic, Gleeson White, "for he has against him all men of infamous life." When the verdict was announced the harlots in the street outside danced upon the pavement.

III

Somewhere about 1450, though later in some parts of Europe by a hundred years or so, and in some earlier, men attained to personality in great numbers, "Unity of Being," and became like a "perfectly proportioned human body," and as men so fashioned held places of power, their nations had it too, prince and ploughman sharing that thought and feeling. What afterwards showed for rifts and cracks were there already, but imperious impulse held all together. Then the scattering came, the seeding of the poppy, bursting of pea-pod, and for a time personality seemed but the stronger for it. Shakespeare's people make all things serve their passion, and that passion is for the moment the whole energy of their being, birds, beasts, men, women, landscape, society, are but symbols and metaphors, nothing is studied in itself, the mind is a dark well, no surface, depth only. The men that Titian painted, the men that Jongsen painted, even the men of Van Dyck, seemed at moments like great hawks at rest. In the Dublin National Gallery there hung, perhaps there still hangs, upon the same wall, a portrait of some Venetian gentleman by Strozzi, and Mr. Sargent's painting of President Wilson. Whatever thought broods in the dark eyes of that Venetian gentleman, has drawn its life from his whole body; it feeds upon it as the flame feeds upon the candle, and should that thought be changed, his pose would change, his very cloak would rustle for his whole body thinks. President Wilson lives only in the eyes, which are steady and intent; the flesh about the mouth is dead, and the hands are dead, and the clothes suggest no movement of his body, nor any movement but that of the valet, who has brushed and folded in mechanical routine. There, all was an energy flowing outward from the nature itself; here, all is the anxious study and slight deflection of external force;

there man's mind and body were predominantly subjective; here all is objective, using those words not as philosophy uses them, but as we use them in conversation.

The bright part of the moon's disk, to adopt the symbolism of a certain poem, is subjective mind, and the dark, objective mind, and we have eight and twenty Phases for our classification of mankind, and of the movement of his thought. At the first Phase, the night where there is no moonlight, all is objective, while when, upon the fifteenth night, the moon comes to the full, there is only subjective mind. The mid-renaissance could but approximate to the full moon "For there is no human life at the full or the dark," but we may attribute to the next three nights of the moon the men of Shakespeare, of Titian, of Strozzi, and of Van Dyck, and watch them grow more reasonable, more orderly, less turbulent, as the nights pass; and it is well to find before the fourth, the nineteenth moon counting from the start, a sudden change, as when a cloud becomes rain, or water freezes, for the great transitions are sudden; popular, typical men have grown more ugly and more argumentative; the face that Van Dyck called a fatal face has faded before Cromwell's warty opinionated head. Henceforth no mind made like "a perfectly proportioned human body" shall sway the public, for great men must live in a portion of themselves, become professional and abstract; but seeing that the moon's third quarter is scarce passed, that abstraction has attained but not passed its climax, that a half, as I affirm it, of the twenty-second night still lingers, they may subdue and conquer; cherish, even, some Utopian dream; spread abstraction ever further till thought is but a film, and there is no dark depth any more, surface only. But men who belong by nature to the nights near to the full are still born, a tragic minority, and how shall they do their work when too ambitious for a private station, except as Wilde of the nineteenth Phase, as my symbolism has it, did his work. He understood his weakness, true personality was impossible, for that is born in solitude, and at his moon one is not solitary; he must project himself before the eyes of others, and, having great ambition, before some great crowd of eyes; but there is no longer any great crowd that cares for his true thought. He must humour and cajole and pose, take worn-out stage situations, for he knows that he may be as romantic as he please, so long as he does not believe in his romance, and all that he may get their ears for a few strokes of contemptuous wit in which he does believe.

We Rhymers did not humour and cajole; but it was not wholly from demerit, it was in part because of different merit, that he refused our exile. Shaw, as I understand him, has no true quarrel with his time, its moon and his almost exactly coincide. He is quite content to exchange Narcissus and his Pool for the signal box at a railway junction, where goods and travellers pass perpetually upon their logical glittering road. Wilde was a monarchist, though content that monarchy should turn demagogue for its own safety, and he held a theatre by the means whereby he held a London dinner table. "He who can dominate a London dinner table," he had boasted, "can dominate the world." While Shaw has but carried his street-corner socialist eloquence on to the stage, and in him one discovers, in his writing and his public speech, as once, before their outline had been softened by prosperity or the passage of the years, in his clothes and in his stiff joints, the civilization that Sargent's picture has explored. Neither his crowd nor he have yet made that discovery that brought President Wilson so near his death, that the moon draws to its fourth quarter. But what happens to the individual man whose moon has come to that fourth quarter, and what to the civilization...?

I can but remember pipe music to-night, though I can half hear beyond it in the memory a weightier music, but this much at any rate is certain, the dream of my early manhood, that a modern nation can return to Unity of Culture, is false; though it may be we can achieve it for some small circle of men and women, and there leave it till the moon bring round its century.

"The cat went here and there
And the moon spun round like a top,

And the nearest kin of the moon
The creeping cat looked up.

Minnaloushe creeps through the grass
From moonlit place to place;
The sacred moon overhead
Has taken a new phase.
Does Minnaloushe know that her pupils
Will pass from change to change,
And that from round to crescent
From crescent to round they range?
Minnaloushe creeps through the grass
Alone, important and wise,
And lifts to the changing moon
Her changing eyes."

IV

Henley's troubles and infirmities were growing upon him. He, too, an ambitious, formidable man,
who showed alike in his practice and in his theory, in his lack of sympathy for Rossetti and Landor,
for instance, that he never understood how small a fragment of our own nature can be brought to
perfect expression, nor that even but with great toil, in a much divided civilization; though,
doubtless, if our own Phase be right, a fragment may be an image of the whole, the moon's still
scarce crumbled image, as it were, in a glass of wine. He would be, and have all poets be, a true
epitome of the whole mass, a Herrick and Dr. Johnson in the same body and because this, not so
difficult before the Mermaid closed its door, is no longer possible, his work lacks music, is abstract,
as even an actor's movement can be when the thought of doing is plainer to his mind than the doing
itself: the straight line from cup to lip, let us say, more plain than the hand's own sensation weighed
down by that heavy spillable cup. I think he was content, when he had called before our eyes, before
the too understanding eyes of his chosen crowd, the violent burly man that he had dreamed,
content with the mere suggestion, and so did not work long enough at his verses. He disliked Victor
Hugo as much as he did Rossetti, and yet Rossetti's translation from Les Burgraves, because of its
mere technical mastery, out-sings Henley in his own song

"My mother is dead; God's patience wears;
It seems my Chaplain will not have done.
Love on: who cares?
Who cares? Love on."

I can read his poetry with emotion, but I read it for some glimpse of what he might have been as
Border balladist, or Cavalier, or of what he actually was, not as poet but as man. He had what Wilde
lacked, even in his ruin, passion, was maybe as passionate as some great man of action, as Parnell,
let us say. When he and Stevenson quarrelled, he cried over it with some woman or other, and his
notorious article was but for vengeance upon Mrs. Stevenson, who had arranged for the public eye,
what he considered an imaginary figure, with no resemblance to the gay companion who had
founded his life, to that life's injury, upon "The august, the immortal musketeers." She had caused
the quarrel, as he believed, and now she had robbed him over again, by blotting from the world's
memory the friend of his youth; and because he believed it I read those angry paragraphs with but
deeper sympathy for the writer; and I think that the man who has left them out of Henley's collected
writings has wronged his memory, as Mrs. Stevenson wronged the memory of Stevenson.

He was no contemplative man, no pleased possessor of wooden models and paper patterns, but a great passionate man, and no friend of his would have him pictured otherwise. I saw little of him in later years, but I doubt if he was ever the same after the death of his six-year old daughter. Few passages of his verse touch me as do those few mentions of her though they lack precision of word and sound. When she is but a hope, he prays that she may have his 'gift of life' and his wife's 'gift of love,' and when she is but a few months old he murmurs over her sleep

When you wake in your crib,
You an inch of experience
Vaulted about
With the wonder of darkness;
Wailing and striving
To reach from your feebleness
Something you feel
Will be good to and cherish you.

And now he commends some friend "boyish and kind, and shy," who greeted him, and greeted his wife, "that day we brought our beautiful one to lie in the green peace" and who is now dead himself, and after that he speaks of love "turned by death to longing" and so, to an enemy.

When I spoke to him of his child's death he said, "she was a person of genius; she had the genius of the mind, and the genius of the body." And later I heard him talk of her as a man talks of something he cannot keep silence over because it is in all his thoughts. I can remember, too, his talking of some book of natural history he had read, that he might be able to answer her questions.

He had a house now at Mortlake on the Thames with a great ivy tod shadowing door and window, and one night there he shocked and startled a roomful of men by showing how far he could be swept beyond our reach in reveries of affection. The dull man, who had tried to put Wilde out of countenance, suddenly said to the whole room, roused by I cannot remember what incautious remark of mine made to some man at my side: "Yeats believes in magic; what nonsense." Henley said, "No, it may not be nonsense; black magic is all the go in Paris now." And then turning towards me with a changed sound in his voice, "It is just a game, isn't it." I replied, not noticing till too late his serious tone, and wishing to avoid discussion in the dull man's company, "One has had a vision; one wants to have another, that is all." Then Henley said, speaking in a very low voice, "I want to know how I am to get to my daughter. I was sitting here the other night when she came into the room and played round the table and went out again. Then I saw that the door was shut and I knew that I had seen a vision." There was an embarrassed silence, and then somebody spoke of something else and we began to discuss it hurriedly and eagerly.

V

I came now to be more in London, never missing the meetings of the Rhymers' Club, nor those of the council of the Irish Literary Society, where I constantly fought out our Irish quarrels and pressed upon the unwilling Gavan Duffy the books of our new movement. The Irish members of Parliament looked upon us with some hostility because we had made it a matter of principle never to put a politician in the chair, and upon other grounds. One day, some old Irish member of Parliament made perhaps his only appearance at a gathering of members. He recited with great emotion a ballad of his own composition in the manner of Young Ireland, repeating over his sacred names, Wolfe Tone, Emmet, and Owen Roe, and mourning that new poets and new movements should have taken something of their sacredness away. The ballad had no literary merit, but I went home with a troubled conscience; and for a dozen years perhaps, till I began to see the result of our work in a deepened perception of all those things that strengthen race, that trouble remained. I had in mind that old politician as I wrote but the other day

"Our part
To murmur name upon name
As a mother names her child."

The Rhymers had begun to break up in tragedy, though we did not know that till the play had finished. I have never found a full explanation of that tragedy; sometimes I have remembered that, unlike the Victorian poets, almost all were poor men, and had made it a matter of conscience to turn from every kind of money-making that prevented good writing, and that poverty meant strain, and for the most part, a refusal of domestic life. Then I have remembered that Johnson had private means, and that others who came to tragic ends, had wives and families. Another day I think that perhaps our form of lyric, our insistence upon emotion which has no relation to any public interest, gathered together, overwrought, unstable men; and remember the moment after that the first to go out of his mind had no lyrical gift, and that we valued him mainly because he seemed a witty man of the world; and that a little later another who seemed, alike as man and writer, dull and formless, went out of his mind, first burning poems which I cannot believe would have proved him as the one man who saw them claims, a man of genius. The meetings were always decorous and often dull; someone would read out a poem and we would comment, too politely for the criticism to have great value; and yet that we read out our poems, and thought that they could be so tested, was a definition of our aims. Love's Nocturne is one of the most beautiful poems in the world, but no one can find out its beauty, so intricate its thought and metaphor, till he has read it over several times, or often stopped his reading to think out the meaning of some passage, and the Faustine of Swinburne, where many separate verses are powerful and musical, could not, were it read out, be understood with pleasure, however clearly it were read, because it has no more logical structure than a bag of shot. I shall, however, remember all my life that evening when Lionel Johnson read or spoke aloud in his musical monotone, where meaning and cadence found the most precise elocution, his poem suggested "by the Statue of King Charles at Charing Cross." It was as though I listened to a great speech. Nor will that poem be to me again what it was that first night. For long I only knew Dowson's O Mors, to quote but the first words of its long title, and his Villanelle of Sunset from his reading, and it was because of the desire to hold them in my hand that I suggested the first Book of The Rhymers' Club. They were not speech but perfect song, though song for the speaking voice. It was perhaps our delight in poetry that was, before all else, speech or song, and could hold the attention of a fitting audience like a good play or good conversation, that made Francis Thompson, whom we admired so much, before the publication of his first poem I had brought to the Cheshire Cheese the proof sheets of his Ode to the Setting Sun, his first published poem, come but once and refuse to contribute to our book. Preoccupied with his elaborate verse, he may have seen only that which we renounced, and thought what seemed to us simplicity, mere emptiness. To some members this simplicity was perhaps created by their tumultuous lives, they praised a desired woman and hoped that she would find amid their praise her very self, or at worst, their very passion; and knew that she, ignoramus that she was, would have slept in the middle of Love's Nocturne, lofty and tender though it be. Woman herself was still in our eyes, for all that, romantic and mysterious, still the priestess of her shrine, our emotions remembering the Lilith and the Sybilla Palmifera of Rossetti; for as yet that sense of comedy, which was soon to mould the very fashion plates, and, in the eyes of men of my generation, to destroy at last the sense of beauty itself, had scarce begun to show here and there, in slight subordinate touches among the designs of great painters and craftsmen. It could not be otherwise, for Johnson's favourite phrase, that life is ritual, expressed something that was in some degree in all our thoughts, and how could life be ritual if woman had not her symbolical place?

If Rossetti was a sub-conscious influence, and perhaps the most powerful of all, we looked consciously to Pater for our philosophy. Three or four years ago I re-read Marius the Epicurean, expecting to find I cared for it no longer, but it still seemed to me, as I think it seemed to us all, the only great prose in modern English, and yet I began to wonder if it, or the attitude of mind of which it was the noblest expression, had not caused the disaster of my friends. It taught us to walk upon a rope, tightly stretched through serene air, and we were left to keep our feet upon a swaying rope in a storm. Pater had made us learned; and, whatever we might be elsewhere, ceremonious and polite, and distant in our relations to one another, and I think none knew as yet that Dowson, who seemed to drink so little and had so much dignity and reserve, was breaking his heart for the daughter of the keeper of an Italian eating house, in dissipation and drink; and that he might that very night sleep upon a sixpenny bed in a doss house. It seems to me that even yet, and I am speaking of 1894 and 1895, we knew nothing of one another, but the poems that we read and criticised; perhaps I have forgotten or was too much in Ireland for knowledge, but of this I am certain, we shared nothing but the artistic life. Sometimes Johnson and Symons would visit our sage at Oxford, and I remember Johnson, whose reports however were not always to be trusted, returning with a sentence that long ran in my head. He had noticed books on political economy among Pater's books, and Pater had said, "Everything that has occupied man, for any length of time, is worthy of our study." Perhaps it was because of Pater's influence that we, with an affectation of learning, claimed the whole past of literature for our authority, instead of finding it like the young men in the age of comedy that followed us, in some new, and so still unrefuted authority; that we preferred what seemed still uncrumbled rock, to the still unspotted foam; that we were traditional alike in our dress, in our manner, in our opinions, and in our style.

Why should men, who spoke their opinions in low voices, as though they feared to disturb the readers in some ancient library, and timidly as though they knew that all subjects had long since been explored, all questions long since decided in books whereon the dust settled, live lives of such disorder and seek to rediscover in verse the syntax of impulsive common life? Was it that we lived in what is called "an age of transition" and so lacked coherence, or did we but pursue antithesis?

VI

All things, apart from love and melancholy, were a study to us; Horne already learned in Botticelli had begun to boast that when he wrote of him there would be no literature, all would be but learning; Symons, as I wrote when I first met him, studied the music halls, as he might have studied the age of Chaucer; while I gave much time to what is called the Christian Cabala; nor was there any branch of knowledge Johnson did not claim for his own. When I had first gone to see him in 1888 or 1889, at the Charlotte Street house, I had called about five in the afternoon, but the man servant that he shared with Horne and Image, told me that he was not yet up, adding with effusion "he is always up for dinner at seven." This habit of breakfasting when others dined had been started by insomnia, but he came to defend it for its own sake. When I asked if it did not separate him from men and women he replied, "In my library I have all the knowledge of the world that I need." He had certainly a considerable library, far larger than that of any young man of my acquaintance, so large that he wondered if it might not be possible to find some way of hanging new shelves from the ceiling like chandeliers. That room was always a pleasure to me, with its curtains of grey corduroy over door and window and book case, and its walls covered with brown paper, a fashion invented, I think, by Horne, that was soon to spread. There was a portrait of Cardinal Newman, looking a little like Johnson himself, some religious picture by Simeon Solomon, and works upon theology in Greek and Latin and a general air of neatness and severity; and talking there by candle light it never seemed very difficult to murmur Villiers de L'isle Adam's proud words, "As for living, our servants will do that for us." Yet I can now see that Johnson himself in some hidden, half-conscious part of him desired the world he had renounced, desired it as an object of study. I was often puzzled as to when and where he could have met the famous men or beautiful women, whose conversation, often wise, and always appropriate, he quoted so often, and it was not till a little before his death that I discovered that these conversations were imaginary. He never altered a detail of speech, and would quote what he had invented for Gladstone or Newman for years without amplification or amendment, with what seemed a scholar's accuracy. His favourite quotations were from Newman, whom, I believe, he had never met, though I can remember nothing now but Newman's greeting to Johnson, "I have always considered the profession of a man of letters a third order of the priesthood!" and these quotations became so well known that at Newman's death, the editor of The Nineteenth Century asked them for publication. Because of his delight in all that was formal and arranged he objected to the public quotation of private conversation even after death, and this scruple helped his refusal. Perhaps this dreaming was made a necessity by his artificial life, yet before that life began he wrote from Oxford to his Tory but flattered family, that as he stood mounted upon a library ladder in his rooms taking a book from a shelf, Gladstone, about to pass the open door on his way upstairs to some college authority, had stopped, hesitated, come into the room and there spent an hour of talk. Presently it was discovered that Gladstone had not been near Oxford on the date given; yet he quoted that conversation without variation of a word until the end of his life, and I think believed in it as firmly as did his friends. These conversations were always admirable in their drama, but never too dramatic or even too polished to lose their casual accidental character; they were the phantasmagoria through which his philosophy of life found its expression. If he made his knowledge of the world out of his phantasy, his knowledge of tongues and books was certainly very great; and yet was that knowledge as great as he would have us believe? Did he really know Welsh, for instance, had he really as he told me, made his only love song, his incomparable Morfydd out of three lines in Welsh, heard sung by a woman at her door on a walking tour in Wales, or did he but wish to hide that he shared in their emotion?

"O, what are the winds?
And what are the waters?
Mine are your eyes."

He wanted us to believe that all things, his poetry with its Latin weight, his religion with its constant reference to the Fathers of the Church, or to the philosophers of the Church, almost his very courtesy were a study and achievement of the intellect. Arthur Symons' poetry made him angry, because it would substitute for that achievement, Parisian impressionism, "a London fog, the blurred tawny lamplight, the red omnibus, the dreary rain, the depressing mud, the glaring gin shop, the slatternly shivering women, three dexterous stanzas telling you that and nothing more." I, on the other hand, angered him by talking as if art existed for emotion only, and for refutation he would quote the close of the Aeschylean Trilogy, the trial of Orestes on the Acropolis. Yet at moments the thought came to him that intellect, as he conceived it, was too much a thing of many books, that it lacked lively experience. "Yeats," he has said to me, "You need ten years in a library, but I have need of ten years in the wilderness." When he said "Wilderness" I am certain, however, that he thought of some historical, some bookish desert, the Thebaid, or the lands about the Mareotic sea. His best poetry is natural and impassioned, but he spoke little of it, but much about his prose, and would contend that I had no right to consider words made to read, less natural than words made to be spoken; and he delighted in a sentence in his book on Thomas Hardy, that kept its vitality, as he contended, though two pages long. He punctuated after the manner of the seventeenth century and was always ready to spend an hour discussing the exact use of the colon. "One should use a colon where other people use a semi-colon, a semi-colon where other people use a comma," was, I think, but a condescension to my ignorance for the matter was plainly beset with many subtleties.

VII

Not till some time in 1895 did I think he could ever drink too much for his sobriety, though what he drank would certainly be too much for that of most of the men whom I knew, I no more doubted his self-control, though we were very intimate friends, than I doubted his memories of Cardinal Newman. The discovery that he did was a great shock to me, and, I think, altered my general view of the world. I had, by my friendship with O'Leary, by my fight against Gavan Duffy, drawn the attention of a group of men, who at that time controlled what remained of the old Fenian movement in England and Scotland; and at a moment when an attempt, that came to nothing, was being made to combine once more our constitutional and unconstitutional politics, I had been asked to represent them at some convention in the United States. I went to consult Johnson, whom I found sitting at a table with books about him. I was greatly tempted, because I was promised complete freedom of speech; and I was at the time enraged by some wild articles published by some Irish American newspaper, suggesting the burning down of the houses of Irish landlords. Nine years later I was lecturing in America, and a charming old Irishman came to see me with an interview to write, and we spent, and as I think in entire neglect of his interview, one of the happiest hours I have ever spent, comparing our tales of the Irish fairies, in which he very firmly believed. When he had gone I looked at his card, to discover that he was the writer of that criminal incitement. I told Johnson that if I had a week to decide in I would probably decide to go, but as they had only given me three days, I had refused. He would not hear of my refusal with so much awaiting my condemnation; and that condemnation would be effective with Catholics, for he would find me passages in the Fathers, condemning every kind of political crime, that of the dynamiter and the incendiary especially. I asked how could the Fathers have condemned weapons they had never heard of, but those weapons, he contended, were merely developments of old methods and weapons; they had decided all in principle; but I need not trouble myself about the matter, for he would put into my hands before I sailed the typewritten statement of their doctrine, dealing with the present situation in the utmost detail. He seemed perfectly logical, but a little more confident and impassioned than usual, and I had, I think, promised to accept, when he rose from his chair, took a step towards me in his eagerness, and fell on to the floor; and I saw that he was drunk. From that on, he began to lose control of his life; he shifted from Charlotte Street, where, I think, there was fear that he would overset lamp or candle and burn the house, to Gray's Inn, and from Gray's Inn to old rambling rooms in Lincoln's Inn Fields, and at last one called to find his outer door shut, the milk on the doorstep sour. Sometimes I would urge him to put himself, as Jack Nettleship had done, into an Institute. One day when I had been very urgent, he spoke of "a craving that made every atom of his body cry out" and said the moment after, "I do not want to be cured," and a moment after that, "In ten years I shall be penniless and shabby, and borrow half-crowns from friends." He seemed to contemplate a vision that gave him pleasure, and now that I look back, I remember that he once said to me that Wilde got, perhaps, an increase of pleasure and excitement from the degradation of that group of beggars and blackmailers where he sought his pathics, and I remember, too, his smile at my surprise, as though he spoke of psychological depths I could never enter. Did the austerity, the melancholy of his thoughts, that spiritual ecstasy which he touched at times, heighten, as complementary colours heighten one another, not only the Vision of Evil, but its fascination? Was it only Villon, or did Dante also feel the fascination of evil, when shown in its horror, and, as it were, judged and lost; and what proud man does not feel temptation strengthened from the certainty that his intellect is not deceived?

VIII

I began now to hear stories of Dowson, whom I knew only at the Rhymers, or through some chance meeting at Johnson's. I was indolent and procrastinating, and when I thought of asking him to dine, or taking some other step towards better knowledge, he seemed to be in Paris, or at Dieppe. He was drinking, but, unlike Johnson, who, at the autopsy after his death, was discovered never to have grown, except in the brain, after his fifteenth year, he was full of sexual desire. Johnson and he were close friends, and Johnson lectured him out of the Fathers upon chastity, and boasted of the great good done him thereby. But the rest of us counted the glasses emptied in their talk. I began to hear now in some detail of the restaurant-keeper's daughter, and of her marriage to the waiter, and of that weekly game of cards with her that filled so great a share of Dowson's emotional life. Sober, he would look at no other woman, it was said, but, drunk, would desire whatever woman chance brought, clean or dirty.

Johnson was stern by nature, strong by intellect, and always, I think, deliberately picked his company, but Dowson seemed gentle, affectionate, drifting. His poetry shows how sincerely he felt the fascination of religion, but his religion had certainly no dogmatic outline, being but a desire for a condition of virginal ecstasy. If it is true, as Arthur Symons, his very close friend, has written, that he loved the restaurant-keeper's daughter for her youth, one may be almost certain that he sought from religion some similar quality, something of that which the angels find who move perpetually, as Swedenborg has said, towards "the dayspring of their youth." Johnson's poetry, like Johnson himself before his last decay, conveys an emotion of joy, of intellectual clearness, of hard energy; he gave us of his triumph; while Dowson's poetry is sad, as he himself seemed, and pictures his life of temptation and defeat,

"Unto us they belong
Us the bitter and gay,
Wine and women and song."

Their way of looking at their intoxication showed their characters. Johnson, who could not have written Dark Angel if he did not suffer from remorse, showed to his friends an impenitent face, and defeated me when I tried to prevent the foundation of an Irish convivial club, it was brought to an end after one meeting by the indignation of the members' wives, whereas the last time I saw Dowson he was pouring out a glass of whiskey for himself in an empty corner of my room and murmuring over and over in what seemed automatic apology "The first to-day."

IX

Two men are always at my side, Lionel Johnson and John Synge whom I was to meet a little later; but Johnson is to me the more vivid in memory, possibly because of the external finish, the clearly-marked lineaments of his body, which seemed but to express the clarity of his mind. I think Dowson's best verse immortal, bound, that is, to outlive famous novels and plays and learned histories and other discursive things, but he was too vague and gentle for my affections. I understood him too well, for I had been like him but for the appetite that made me search out strong condiments. Though I cannot explain what brought others of my generation to such misfortune, I think that (falling backward upon my parable of the moon) I can explain some part of Dowson's and Johnson's dissipation

"What portion in the world can the artist have,
Who has awaked from the common dream,
But dissipation and despair?"

When Edmund Spencer described the islands of Phaedria and of Acrasia he aroused the indignation of Lord Burleigh, "that rugged forehead" and Lord Burleigh was in the right if morality were our only object.

In those islands certain qualities of beauty, certain forms of sensuous loveliness were separated from all the general purposes of life, as they had not been hitherto in European literature, and would not be again, for even the historical process has its ebb and flow, till Keats wrote his Endymion. I think that the movement of our thought has more and more so separated certain images and regions of the mind, and that these images grow in beauty as they grow in sterility. Shakespeare leaned, as it were, even as craftsman, upon the general fate of men and nations, had about him the excitement of the playhouse; and all poets, including Spencer in all but a few pages, until our age came, and when it came almost all, have had some propaganda or traditional doctrine to give companionship with their fellows. Had not Matthew Arnold his faith in what he described as the best thought of his generation? Browning his psychological curiosity, Tennyson, as before him Shelley and Wordsworth, moral values that were not aesthetic values? But Coleridge of the Ancient Mariner, and Kubla Khan, and Rossetti in all his writings made what Arnold has called that "morbid effort," that search for "perfection of thought and feeling, and to unite this to perfection of form," sought this new, pure beauty, and suffered in their lives because of it. The typical men of the classical age (I think of Commodus, with his half-animal beauty, his cruelty, and his caprice), lived public lives, pursuing curiosities of appetite, and so found in Christianity, with its Thebaid and its Mariotic Sea the needed curb. But what can the Christian confessor say to those who more and more must make all out of the privacy of their thought, calling up perpetual images of desire, for he cannot say "Cease to be artist, cease to be poet," where the whole life is art and poetry, nor can he bid men leave the world, who suffer from the terrors that pass before shut-eyes. Coleridge, and Rossetti though his dull brother did once persuade him that he was an agnostic, were devout Christians, and Steinbock and Beardsley were so towards their lives' end, and Dowson and Johnson always, and yet I think it but deepened despair and multiplied temptation.

"Dark Angel, with thine aching lust,
To rid the world of penitence:
Malicious angel, who still dost
My soul such subtil violence!

When music sounds, then changest thou
A silvery to a sultry fire:
Nor will thine envious heart allow
Delight untortured by desire.

Through thee, the gracious Muses turn
To Furies, O mine Enemy!
And all the things of beauty burn
With flames of evil ecstasy.

Because of thee, the land of dreams
Becomes a gathering place of fears:
Until tormented slumber seems
One vehemence of useless tears."

Why are these strange souls born everywhere to-day? with hearts that Christianity, as shaped by history, cannot satisfy. Our love letters wear out our love; no school of painting outlasts its founders, every stroke of the brush exhausts the impulse, Pre-Raphaelitism had some twenty years;

impressionism thirty perhaps. Why should we believe that religion can never bring round its antithesis? Is it true that our air is disturbed, as Malarmé said, by "the trembling of the veil of the temple," or "that our whole age is seeking to bring forth a sacred book?" Some of us thought that book near towards the end of last century, but the tide sank again.

X

I do not know whether John Davidson, whose life also was tragic, made that "morbid effort," that search for "perfection of thought and feeling," for he is hidden behind failure, to unite it "to perfection of form." At eleven one morning I met him in the British Museum reading room, probably in 1894, when I was in London for the production of The Land of Heart's Desire, but certainly after some long absence from London. "Are you working here?" I said; "No," he said, "I am loafing, for I have finished my day's work." "What, already?" "I work an hour a day, I cannot work longer without exhaustion, and even as it is, if I meet anybody and get into talk, I cannot write the next day; that is why I loaf when my work is finished." No one had ever doubted his industry; he had supported his wife and family for years by "devilling" many hours a day for some popular novelist. "What work is it?" I said. "I am writing verse," he answered. "I had been writing prose for a long time, and then one day I thought I might just as well write what I liked, as I must starve in any case. It was the luckiest thought I ever had, for my agent now gets me forty pounds for a ballad, and I made three hundred out of my last book of verse."

He was older by ten years than his fellow Rhymers; a national schoolmaster from Scotland, he had been dismissed, he told us, for asking for a rise in his salary, and had come to London with his wife and children. He looked older than his years. "Ellis," he had said, "how old are you?" "Fifty," Edwin Ellis replied, or whatever his age was. "Then I will take off my wig. I never take off my wig when there is a man under thirty in the room." He had endured and was to endure again, a life of tragic penury, which was made much harder by the conviction that the world was against him, that he was refused for some reason his rightful position. Ellis thought that he pined even for social success, and I that his Scots jealousy kept him provincial and but half articulate.

During the quarrel over Parnell's grave a quotation from Goethe ran through the papers, describing our Irish jealousy: "The Irish seem to me like a pack of hounds, always dragging down some noble stag." But I do not think we object to distinction for its own sake; if we kill the stag, it is that we may carry off his head and antlers. "The Irish people," O'Leary used to say, "do not know good from bad in any art, but they do not hate the good once it is pointed out to them because it is good." An infallible Church, with its Mass in Latin, and its mediaeval philosophy, and our Protestant social prejudice, have kept our ablest men from levelling passions; but Davidson with a jealousy, which may be Scottish, seeing that Carlyle had it, was quick to discover sour grapes. He saw in delicate, laborious, discriminating taste, an effeminate pedantry, and would, when that mood was on him, delight in all that seemed healthy, popular, and bustling. Once when I had praised Herbert Horne for his knowledge and his taste, he burst out, "If a man must be a connoisseur, let him be a connoisseur in women." He, indeed, was accustomed, in the most characteristic phrase of his type, to describe the Rhymers as lacking in "blood and guts," and very nearly brought us to an end by attempting to supply the deficiency by the addition of four Scotsmen. He brought all four upon the same evening, and one read out a poem upon the Life Boat, evidently intended for a recitation; another described how, when gold-digging in Australia, he had fought and knocked down another miner for doubting the rotundity of the earth; while of the remainder I can remember nothing except that they excelled in argument. He insisted upon their immediate election, and the Rhymers, through that complacency of good manners whereby educated Englishmen so often surprise me, obeyed, though secretly resolved never to meet again; and it cost me seven hours' work to get another meeting, and vote the Scotsmen out. A few days later I chanced upon Davidson at some restaurant; he was full of amiability, and when we parted shook my hand, and proclaimed enthusiastically that I had "blood and guts." I think he might have grown to be a successful man had he been enthusiastic instead about Dowson or Johnson, or Horne or Symons, for they had what I still lacked, conscious deliberate craft, and what I must lack always, scholarship. They had taught me that violent energy, which is like a fire of straw, consumes in a few minutes the nervous vitality, and is useless in the arts. Our fire must burn slowly, and we must constantly turn away to think, constantly analyse what we have done, be content even to have little life outside our work, to show, perhaps, to other men, as little as the watch-mender shows, his magnifying glass caught in his screwed-up eye. Only then do we learn to conserve our vitality, to keep our mind enough under control and to make our technique sufficiently flexible for expression of the emotions of life as they arise. A few months after our meeting in the Museum, Davidson had spent his inspiration. "The fires are out," he said, "and I must hammer the cold iron." When I heard a few years ago that he had drowned himself, I knew that I had always expected some such end. With enough passion to make a great poet, through meeting no man of culture in early life, he lacked intellectual receptivity, and, anarchic and indefinite, lacked pose and gesture, and now no verse of his clings to my memory.

XI

Gradually Arthur Symons came to replace in my intimate friendship, Lionel Johnson from whom I was slowly separated by a scruple of conscience. If he came to see me he sat tongue-tied unless I gave him the drink that seemed necessary to bring his vitality to but its normal pitch, and if I called upon him he drank so much that I became his confederate. Once, when a friend and I had sat long after our proper bed-time at his constantly repeated and most earnest entreaty, knowing what black melancholy would descend upon him at our departure, and with the unexpressed hope of getting him to his bed, he fixed upon us a laughing and whimsical look, and said: "I want you two men to understand that you are merely two men that I am drinking with." That was the only time that I was to hear from him an imaginary conversation that had not an air of the most scrupulous accuracy. He gave two accounts of a conversation with Wilde in prison; in one Wilde wore his hair long, and in the other it had been cropped by the prison barber. He was gradually losing, too, the faculty of experience, and in his prose and verse repeated the old ideas and emotions, but faintly, as though with fading interest. I am certain that he prayed much, and on those rare days that I came upon him dressed and active before midday or but little after, I concluded that he had been to morning Mass at Farm Street.

When with Johnson I had tuned myself to his mood, but Arthur Symons, more than any man I have ever known, could slip as it were into the mind of another, and my thoughts gained in richness and in clearness from his sympathy, nor shall I ever know how much my practice and my theory owe to the passages that he read me from Catullus and from Verlaine and Mallarmé. I had read Axel to myself or was still reading it, so slowly, and with so much difficulty, that certain passages had an exaggerated importance, while all remained so obscure that I could without much effort imagine that here at last was the Sacred Book I longed for. An Irish friend of mine lives in a house where beside a little old tower rises a great new Gothic hall and stair, and I have sometimes got him to extinguish all light but a little Roman lamp, and in that faint light and among great vague shadows, blotting away the unmeaning ornament, have imagined myself partaking in some incredible romance. Half-a-dozen times, beginning in boyhood with Shelley's Prometheus Unbound, I have in that mood possessed for certain hours or months the book that I long for; and Symons, without ever being false to his own impressionist view of art and of life, deepened as I think my longing.

It seems to me, looking backward, that we always discussed life at its most intense moment, that moment which gives a common sacredness to the Song of Songs, and to the Sermon on the Mount, and in which one discovers something supernatural, a stirring as it were of the roots of the hair. He was making those translations from Mallarmé and from Verlaine, from Calderon, from St. John of the Cross, which are the most accomplished metrical translations of our time, and I think that those from Mallarmé may have given elaborate form to my verses of those years, to the latter poems of The Wind Among the Reeds, to The Shadowy Waters, while Villiers de L'Isle Adam had shaped whatever in my Rosa Alchemica Pater had not shaped. I can remember the day in Fountain Court when he first read me Herodiade's address to some Sibyl who is her nurse and it may be the moon also:

"The horror of my virginity
Delights me, and I would envelope me
In the terror of my tresses, that, by night,
Inviolate reptile, I might feel the white
And glimmering radiance of thy frozen fire,
Thou that art chaste and diest of desire,
White night of ice and of the cruel snow!
Eternal sister, my lone sister, lo
My dreams uplifted before thee! now, apart,
So rare a crystal is my dreaming heart,
And all about me lives but in mine own
Image, the idolatrous mirror of my pride,
Mirroring this Herodiade diamond-eyed."

Yet I am certain that there was something in myself compelling me to attempt creation of an art as separate from everything heterogenous and casual, from all character and circumstance, as some Herodiade of our theatre, dancing seemingly alone in her narrow moving luminous circle. Certainly I had gone a great distance from my first poems, from all that I had copied from the folk-art of Ireland, as from the statue of Mausolus and his Queen, where the luminous circle is motionless and contains the entire popular life; and yet why am I so certain? I can imagine an Aran Islander who had strayed into the Luxembourg Gallery, turning bewildered from Impressionist or Post-Impressionist, but lingering at Moreau's "Jason," to study in minute astonishment the elaborate background, where there are so many jewels, so much wrought stone and moulded bronze. Had not lover promised mistress in his own island song, "A ship with a gold and silver mast, gloves of the skin of a fish, and shoes of the skin of a bird, and a suit of the dearest silk in Ireland?"

XII

Hitherto when in London I had stayed with my family in Bedford Park, but now I was to live for some twelve months in chambers in the Temple that opened through a little passage into those of Arthur Symons. If anybody rang at either door, one or other would look through a window in the connecting passage, and report. We would then decide whether one or both should receive the visitor, whether his door or mine should be opened, or whether both doors were to remain closed. I have never liked London, but London seemed less disagreeable when one could walk in quiet, empty places after dark, and upon a Sunday morning sit upon the margin of a fountain almost as alone as if in the country. I was already settled there, I imagine, when a publisher called and proposed that Symons should edit a Review or Magazine, and Symons consented on the condition that Beardsley were Art Editor and I was delighted at his condition as I think were all his other proposed contributors. Aubrey Beardsley had been dismissed from the Art editorship of The Yellow Book under circumstances that had made us indignant. He had illustrated Wilde's Salome, his strange satiric art had raised the popular press to fury, and at the height of the excitement aroused by Wilde's condemnation, a popular novelist, a woman who had great influence among the most conventional part of the British public, had written demanding his dismissal. "She owed it to her position before the British people," she had said. Beardsley was not even a friend of Wilde's, they even disliked each other, he had no sexual abnormality, but he was certainly unpopular, and the moment had come to get rid of unpopular persons. The public at once concluded, they could hardly conclude otherwise, he was dismissed by telegram, that there was evidence against him, and Beardsley, who was some twenty-three years old, being embittered and miserable, plunged into dissipation. We knew that we must face an infuriated press and public, but being all young we delighted in enemies and in everything that had an heroic air.

XIII

We might have survived but for our association with Beardsley, perhaps, but for his Under the Hill, a Rabelaisian fragment promising a literary genius as great maybe as his artistic genius, and for the refusal of the bookseller who controlled the railway bookstalls to display our wares. The bookseller's manager, no doubt looking for a design of Beardsley's, pitched upon Blake's Anteus setting Virgil and Dante upon the verge of Cocytus as the ground of refusal, and when Arthur Symons pointed out that Blake was considered "a very spiritual artist" replied, "O, Mr Symons, you must remember that we have an audience of young ladies as well as an audience of agnostics." However, he called Arthur Symons back from the door to say, "If contrary to our expectations The Savoy should have a large sale, we should be very glad to see you again." As Blake's design illustrated an article of mine, I wrote a letter upon that remarkable saying to a principal daily newspaper. But I had mentioned Beardsley, and I was told that the editor had made it a rule that his paper was never to mention Beardsley's name. I said upon meeting him later, "Would you have made the same rule in the case of Hogarth?" against whom much the same objection could be taken, and he replied with what seemed to me a dreamy look, as though suddenly reminded of a lost opportunity, "Ah, there was no popular press in Hogarth's day." We were not allowed to forget that in our own day there was a popular press, and its opinions began to affect our casual acquaintance, and even our comfort in public places. At some well-known house, an elderly man to whom I had just been introduced, got up from my side and walked to the other end of the room; but it was as much my reputation as an Irish rebel as the evil company that I was supposed to keep, that excited some young men in a railway carriage to comment upon my general career in voices raised that they might catch my attention. I discovered, however, one evening that we were perhaps envied as well as despised. I was in the pit at some theatre, and had just noticed Arthur Symons a little in front of me, when I heard a young man, who looked like a shop-assistant or clerk, say, "There is Arthur Symons. If he can't get an order, why can't he pay for a stall." Clearly we were supposed to prosper upon iniquity, and to go to the pit added a sordid parsimony. At another theatre I caught sight of a woman that I once liked, the widow of some friend of my father's youth, and tried to attract her attention, but she had no eyes for anything but the stage curtain; and at some house where I met no hostility to myself, a popular novelist snatched out of my hand a copy of The Savoy, and opening it at Beardsley's drawing, called The Barber, began to expound its bad drawing and wound up with, "Now if you want to admire really great black and white art, admire the Punch Cartoons of Mr Lindley Sambourne," and our hostess, after making peace between us, said, "O, Mr Yeats, why do you not send your poems to The Spectator instead of to The Savoy." The answer, "My friends read the Savoy and they do not read The Spectator," brought a look of deeper disapproval.

Yet, even apart from Beardsley, we were a sufficiently distinguished body: Max Beerbohm, Bernard Shaw, Ernest Dowson, Lionel Johnson, Arthur Symons, Charles Conder, Charles Shannon, Havelock

Ellis, Selwyn Image, Joseph Conrad; but nothing counted but the one hated name. I think that had we been challenged we might have argued something after this fashion: "Science through much ridicule and some persecution has won its right to explore whatever passes before its corporeal eye, and merely because it passes: to set as it were upon an equality the beetle and the whale though Ben Jonson could find no justification for the entomologist in The New Inn, but that he had been crossed in love. Literature now demands the same right of exploration of all that passes before the mind's eyes, and merely because it passes." Not a complete defence, for it substitutes a spiritual for a physical objective, but sufficient it may be for the moment, and to settle our place in the historical process.

The critic might well reply that certain of my generation delighted in writing with an unscientific partiality for subjects long forbidden. Yet is it not most important to explore especially what has been long forbidden, and to do this not only "with the highest moral purpose," like the followers of Ibsen, but gaily, out of sheer mischief, or sheer delight in that play of the mind. Donne could be as metaphysical as he pleased, and yet never seemed unhuman and hysterical as Shelley often does, because he could be as physical as he pleased; and besides who will thirst for the metaphysical, who have a parched tongue, if we cannot recover the Vision of Evil?

I have felt in certain early works of my own which I have long abandoned, and here and there in the work of others of my generation, a slight, sentimental sensuality which is disagreeable, and doesn't exist in the work of Donne, let us say, because he, being permitted to say what he pleased, was never tempted to linger, or rather to pretend that we can linger, between spirit and sense. How often had I heard men of my time talk of the meeting of spirit and sense, yet there is no meeting but only change upon the instant, and it is by the perception of a change like the sudden "blacking out" of the lights of the stage, that passion creates its most violent sensation.

XIV

Dowson was now at Dieppe, now at a Normandy village. Wilde, too, was at Dieppe; and Symons, Beardsley, and others would cross and recross, returning with many tales, and there were letters and telegrams. Dowson wrote a protest against some friend's too vivid essay upon the disorder of his life, and explained that in reality he was living a life of industry in a little country village; but before the letter arrived that friend received a wire, "arrested, sell watch and send proceeds." Dowson's watch had been left in London and then another wire, "Am free." Dowson, ran the tale as I heard it ten years after, had got drunk and fought the baker, and a deputation of villagers had gone to the magistrate and pointed out that Monsieur Dowson was one of the most illustrious of English poets. "Quite right to remind me," said the magistrate, "I will imprison the baker."

A Rhymer had seen Dowson at some cafe in Dieppe with a particularly common harlot, and as he passed, Dowson, who was half drunk, caught him by the sleeve and whispered, "She writes poetry, it is like Browning and Mrs Browning." Then there came a wonderful tale, repeated by Dowson himself, whether by word of mouth or by letter I do not remember. Wilde has arrived in Dieppe, and Dowson presses upon him the necessity of acquiring "a more wholesome taste." They empty their pockets on to the café table, and though there is not much, there is enough if both heaps are put into one. Meanwhile the news has spread, and they set out accompanied by a cheering crowd. Arrived at their destination, Dowson and the crowd remain outside, and presently Wilde returns. He says in a low voice to Dowson, "The first these ten years, and it will be the last. It was like cold mutton", always, as Henley had said, "a scholar and a gentleman," he no doubt remembered the sense in which the Elizabethan dramatists used the words "Cold mutton", and then aloud so that the crowd may hear him, "But tell it in England, for it will entirely restore my character."

XV

When the first few numbers of The Savoy had been published, the contributors and the publisher gave themselves a supper, and Symons explained that certain among us were invited afterwards to the publisher's house, and if I went there that once I need never go again. I considered the publisher a scandalous person, and had refused to meet him; we were all agreed as to his character, and only differed as to the distance that should lie between him and us. I had just received two letters, one from T. W. Rolleston protesting with all the conventional moral earnestness of an article in The Spectator newspaper, against my writing for such a magazine; and one from A. E. denouncing that magazine, which he called the "Organ of the Incubi and the Succubi," with the intensity of a personal conviction. I had forgotten that Arthur Symons had borrowed the letters until as we stood about the supper table waiting for the signal to be seated, I heard the infuriated voice of the publisher shouting, "Give me the letter, give me the letter, I will prosecute that man," and I saw Symons waving Rolleston's letter just out of reach. Then Symons folded it up and put it in his pocket, and began to read out A. E. and the publisher was silent, and I saw Beardsley listening. Presently Beardsley came to me and said, "Yeats, I am going to surprise you very much. I think your friend is right. All my life I have been fascinated by the spiritual life, when a child I saw a vision of a Bleeding Christ over the mantelpiece, but after all to do one's work when there are other things one wants to do so much more, is a kind of religion."

Something, I forget what, delayed me a few minutes after the supper was over, and when I arrived at our publisher's I found Beardsley propped up on a chair in the middle of the room, grey and exhausted, and as I came in he left the chair and went into another room to spit blood, but returned immediately. Our publisher, perspiration pouring from his face, was turning the handle of a hurdy gurdy piano, it worked by electricity, I was told, when the company did not cut off the supply, and very plainly had had enough of it, but Beardsley pressed him to labour on, "The tone is so beautiful," "It gives me such deep pleasure," etc., etc. It was his method of keeping our publisher at a distance.

Another image competes with that image in my memory. Beardsley has arrived at Fountain Court a little after breakfast with a young woman who belongs to our publisher's circle and certainly not to ours, and is called "twopence coloured," or is it "penny plain." He is a little drunk and his mind has been running upon his dismissal from The Yellow Book, for he puts his hand upon the wall and stares into a mirror. He mutters, "Yes, yes. I look like a Sodomite," which he certainly did not. "But no, I am not that," and then begins railing, against his ancestors, accusing them of that and this, back to and including the great Pitt, from whom he declares himself descended.

XVI

I can no more justify my convictions in these brief chapters, where I touch on fundamental things, than Shakespeare could justify within the limits of a sonnet, his conviction that the soul of the wide world dreams of things to come; and yet as I have set out to describe nature as I see it, I must not only describe events but those patterns into which they fall, when I am the looker-on. A French miracle-working priest once said to Maud Gonne and myself and to an English Catholic who had come with us, that a certain holy woman had been the "victim" for his village, and that another holy woman who had been "victim" for all France, had given him her Crucifix, because he, too, was doomed to become a "victim."

French psychical research has offered evidence to support the historical proofs that such saints as Lydwine of Schiedam, whose life suggested to Paul Claudel his L'Annonce faite à Marie, did really cure disease by taking it upon themselves. As disease was considered the consequence of sin, to take it upon themselves was to copy Christ. All my proof that mind flows into mind, and that we cannot separate mind and body, drives me to accept the thought of victimage in many complex forms, and I ask myself if I cannot so explain the strange, precocious genius of Beardsley. He was in my Lunar metaphor a man of the thirteenth Phase, his nature on the edge of Unity of Being, the understanding of that Unity by the intellect his one overmastering purpose; whereas Lydwine de Schiedam and her like, being of the saints, are at the seven and twentieth Phase, and seek a unity with a life beyond individual being; and so being all subjective he would take upon himself not the consequences, but the knowledge of sin. I surrender myself to the wild thought that by so doing he enabled persons who had never heard his name, to recover innocence. I have so often, too, practised meditations, or experienced dreams, where the meditations or dreams of two or three persons contrast and complement one another, in so far as those persons are in themselves complementary or contrasting, that I am convinced that it is precisely from the saint or potential saint that he would gather this knowledge. I see in his fat women and shadowy, pathetic girls, his horrible children, half child, half embryo, in all the lascivious monstrous imagery of the privately published designs, the phantasms that from the beginning have defied the scourge and the hair shirt. I once said to him half seriously, "Beardsley, I was defending you last night in the only way in which it is possible to defend you, by saying that all you draw is inspired by rage against iniquity," and he answered, "If it were so inspired the work would be in no way different," meaning, as I think, that he drew with such sincerity that no change of motive could change the image.

I know that some turn of disease had begun to parade erotic images before his eyes, and I do not doubt that he drew these images. "I make a blot upon the paper," he said to me; "And I begin to shove the ink about and something comes." But I was wrong to say that he drew these things in rage against iniquity, for to know that rage he must needs be objective, concerned with other people, with the Church or the Divinity, with something outside his own head, and responsible not for the knowledge but for the consequence of sin. His preparation had been the exhaustion of sin in act, while the preparation of the Saint is the exhaustion of his pride, and instead of the Saint's humility, he had come to see the images of the mind in a kind of frozen passion, the virginity of the intellect.

Does not all art come when a nature, that never ceases to judge itself, exhausts personal emotion in action or desire so completely that something impersonal, something that has nothing to do with action or desire, suddenly starts into its place, something which is as unforeseen, as completely organized, even as unique, as the images that pass before the mind between sleeping and waking.

But all art is not victimage; and much of the hatred of the art of Beardsley came from the fact that victimage, though familiar under another name to French criticism since the time of Baudelaire, was not known in England. He pictures almost always disillusion, and apart from those privately published drawings which he tried upon his deathbed to have destroyed, there is no representation of desire. Even the beautiful women are exaggerated into doll-like prettiness by a spirit of irony, or are poignant with a thwarted or corrupted innocence. I see his art with more understanding now, than when he lived, for in 1895 or 1896, I was in despair at the new breath of comedy that had begun to wither the beauty that I loved, just when that beauty seemed about to unite itself to mystery. I said to him once, "You have never done anything to equal your Salome with the head of John the Baptist." I think, that for the moment he was sincere when he replied, "Yes, yes; but beauty is so difficult." It was for the moment only, for as the popular rage increased and his own disease increased, he became more and more violent in his satire, or created out of a spirit of mockery a form of beauty where his powerful logical intellect eliminated every outline that suggested meditation or even satisfied passion.

The distinction between the Image, between the apparition as it were, and the personal action and desire, took a new form at the approach of death. He made two or three charming and blasphemous designs; I think especially of a Madonna and Child, where the Child has a foolish, doll-like face, and an elaborate modern baby's dress; and of a St. Rose of Lima in an expensive gown decorated with roses, ascending to Heaven upon the bosom of the Madonna, her face enraptured with love, but with that form of it which is least associated with sanctity. I think that his conversion to Catholicism was sincere, but that so much of impulse as could exhaust itself in prayer and ceremony, in formal action and desire, found itself mocked by the antithetical image; and yet I am perhaps mistaken, perhaps it was merely his recognition that historical Christianity had dwindled to a box of toys, and that it might be amusing to empty the whole box on to the counterpane.

XVII

I had been a good deal in Paris, though never very long at any time, my later visits with a member of the Rhymer's Club whose curiosity or emotion was roused by every pretty girl. He treated me with a now admiring, now mocking wonder, because being in love, and in no way lucky in that love, I had grown exceedingly puritanical so far as my immediate neighbourhood was concerned. One night, close to the Luxembourg, a strange young woman in bicycling costume, came out of a side street, threw one arm about his neck, walked beside us in perfect silence for a hundred yards or so, and then darted up another side street. He had a red and white complexion and fair hair, but how she discovered that in the dark I could not understand. I became angry and reproachful, but he defended himself by saying, "You never meet a stray cat without caressing it: I have similar instincts." Presently we found ourselves at some Café, the Café D'Harcourt, I think, and when I looked up from my English newspaper, I found myself surrounded with painted ladies and saw that he was taking vengeance. I could not have carried on a conversation in French, but I was able to say, "That gentleman over there has never refused wine or coffee to any lady," and in a little they had all settled about him like greedy pigeons.

I had put my ideal of those years, an ideal that passed away with youth, into my description of Proud Costello. "He was of those ascetics of passion, who keep their hearts pure for love or for hatred, as other men for God, for Mary and for the Saints." My friend was not interested in passion. A woman drew him to her by some romantic singularity in her beauty or her circumstance, and drew him the more if the curiosity she aroused were half intellectual. A little after the time I write of, throwing himself into my chair after some visit to a music-hall or hippodrome, he began, "O, Yeats, I was never in love with a serpent-charmer before." He was objective. For him "the visible world existed" as he was fond of quoting, and I suspect him of a Moon that had entered its fourth quarter.

XVIII

At first I used to stay with Macgregor Mathers and his gracious young wife near the Champ de Mars, or in the Rue Mozart, but later by myself in a student's hotel in the Latin quarter, and I cannot remember always where I stayed when this or that event took place. Macgregor Mathers, or Macgregor, for he had now shed the "Mathers," would come down to breakfast one day with his Horace, the next day with his Macpherson's Ossian, and read out fragments during breakfast, considering both books of equal authenticity. Once when I questioned that of Ossian, he got into a rage, what right had I to take sides with the English enemy, and I found that for him the eighteenth century controversy still raged. At night he would dress himself in Highland dress, and dance the sword dance, and his mind brooded upon the ramifications of clans and tartans. Yet I have at moments doubted whether he had seen the Highlands, or even, until invited there by some White Rose Society, Scotland itself. Every Sunday he gave to the evocation of Spirits, and I noted that upon that day he would spit blood. That did not matter, he said, because it came from his head, not his lungs; what ailed him I do not know, but I think that he lived under some great strain, and presently I noted that he was drinking neat brandy, not to drunkenness, but to detriment of mind and body.

He began to foresee changes in the world, announcing in 1893 or 1894, the imminence of immense wars, and was it in 1895 or 1896 that he learned ambulance work, and made others learn it? He had a sabre wound on his wrist, or perhaps his forehead, for my memory is not clear, got in some student riot that he had mistaken for the beginning of war. It may have been some talk of his that made me write the poem that begins:

"The dews drop slowly and dreams gather; unknown spears
Suddenly hurtle before my dream awakened eyes,
And then the clash of fallen horsemen and the cries
Of unknown perishing armies beat about my ears."

War was to bring, or be brought by, anarchy, but that would be a passing stage, he declared, for his dreams were all Napoleonic. He certainly foresaw some great role that he could play, had made himself an acknowledged master of the war-game, and for a time taught it to French officers for his living. He was to die of melancholia, and was perhaps already mad at certain moments or upon certain topics, though he did not make upon me that impression in those early days, being generous, gay, and affable. I have seen none that lacked philosophy and trod Hodos Camelionis come to good there; and he lacked it but for a vague affirmation, that he would have his friends affirm also, each for himself, "There is no part of me that is not of the Gods." Once, when he had told me that he met his Teachers in some great crowd, and only knew that they were phantoms by a shock that was like an electric shock to his heart, I asked him how he knew that he was not deceived or hallucinated. He said, "I had been visited by one of them the other night, and I followed him out, and followed him down that little lane to the right. Presently I fell over the milk boy, and the milk boy got in a rage because he said that not only I but the man in front had fallen over him." He like all that I have known, who have given themselves up to images, and to the murmuring of images, thought that when he had proved that an image could act independently of his mind, he had proved also that neither it, nor what it had murmured, had originated there. Yet had I need of proof to the contrary, I had it while under his roof. I was eager for news of the Spanish-American war, and went to the Rue Mozart before breakfast to buy a New York Herald. As I went out past the young Normandy servant who was laying breakfast, I was telling myself some schoolboy romance, and had just reached a place where I carried my arm in a sling after some remarkable escape. I bought my paper and returned, to find Macgregor on the doorstep. "Why, you are all right," he said, "What did the Bonne mean by telling me that you had hurt your arm and carried it in a sling."

Once when I met him in the street in his Highland clothes, with several knives in his stocking, he said, "When I am dressed like this I feel like a walking flame," and I think that everything he did was but an attempt to feel like a walking flame. Yet at heart he was, I think, gentle, and perhaps even a little timid. He had some impediment in his nose that gave him a great deal of trouble, and it could have been removed had he not shrunk from the slight operation; and once when he was left in a mouse-infested flat with some live traps, he collected his captives into a large birdcage, and to avoid the necessity of their drowning, fed them there for weeks. Being a self-educated, un-scholarly, though learned man, he was bound to express the fundamental antithesis in the most crude form, and being arrogant, to prevent as far as possible that alternation between the two natures which is, it may be, necessary to sanity. When the nature turns to its spiritual opposite alone there can be no alternation, but what nature is pure enough for that.

I see Paris in the Eighteen-nineties as a number of events separated from one another, and without cause or consequence, without lot or part in the logical structure of my life; I can often as little find their dates as I can those of events in my early childhood. William Sharp, who came to see me there, may have come in 1895, or on some visit four or five years later, but certainly I was in an hotel in the Boulevard Raspail. When he stood up to go he said, "What is that?" pointing to a geometrical form painted upon a little piece of cardboard that lay upon my window sill. And then before I could answer, looked out of the window saying, "There is a funeral passing." I said, "That is curious, as the Death symbol is painted upon the card." I did not look, but I am sure there was no funeral. A few days later he came back and said, "I have been very ill; you must never allow me to see that symbol again." He did not seem anxious to be questioned, but years later he said, "I will now tell you what happened in Paris. I had two rooms at my hotel, a front sitting-room and a bedroom leading out of it. As I passed the threshold of the sitting-room, I saw a woman standing at the bureau writing, and presently she went into my bedroom. I thought somebody had got into the wrong room by mistake, but when I went to the bureau I saw the sheet of paper she had seemed to write upon, and there was no writing upon it. I went into my bed-room and I found nobody, but as there was a door from the bedroom on to the stairs I went down the stairs to see if she had gone that way. When I got out into the street I saw her just turning a corner, but when I turned the corner there was nobody there, and then I saw her at another corner. Constantly seeing her and losing her like that I followed till I came to the Seine, and there I saw her standing at an opening in the wall, looking down into the river. Then she vanished, and I cannot tell why, but I went to the opening in the wall and stood there, just as she had stood, taking just the same attitude. Then I thought I was in Scotland, and that I heard a sheep bell. After that I must have lost consciousness, for I knew nothing till I found myself lying on my back, dripping wet, and people standing all round. I had thrown myself into the Seine."

I did not believe him, and not because I thought the story impossible, for I knew he had a susceptibility beyond that of any one I had ever known, to symbolic or telepathic influence, but because he never told one anything that was true; the facts of life disturbed him and were forgotten. The story had been created by the influence but it had remained a reverie, though he may in the course of years have come to believe that it happened as an event. The affectionate husband of his admiring and devoted wife, he had created an imaginary beloved, had attributed to her the authorship of all his books that had any talent, and though habitually a sober man, I have known him to get drunk, and at the height of his intoxication when most men speak the truth, to attribute his state to remorse for having been unfaithful to Fiona Macleod.

Paul Verlaine alternated between the two halves of his nature with so little apparent resistance that he seemed like a bad child, though to read his sacred poems is to remember perhaps that the Holy Infant shared His first home with the beasts. In what month was it that I received a note inviting me to "coffee and cigarettes plentifully," and signed "Yours quite cheerfully, Paul Verlaine?" I found him at the top of a tenement house in the Rue St. Jacques, sitting in an easy chair, his bad leg swaddled in many bandages. He asked me, speaking in English, if I knew Paris well, and added, pointing to his leg, that it had scorched his leg for he know it "well, too well" and "lived in it like a fly in a pot of marmalade." He took up an English dictionary, one of the few books in the room, and began searching for the name of his disease, selecting after a long search and with, as I understood, only comparative accuracy "Erysipelas." Meanwhile his homely, middle-aged mistress made the coffee and found the cigarettes; it was obviously she who had given the room its character; her canaries in several cages hanging in the window, and her sentimental lithographs nailed here and there among the nude drawings and newspaper caricatures of her lover as various kinds of monkey, which he had pinned upon the wall. A slovenly, ragged man came in, his trousers belted with a piece of rope and an opera hat upon his head. She drew a box over to the fire, and he sat down, now holding the opera hat upon his knees, and I think he must have acquired it very lately for he kept constantly closing and opening it. Verlaine introduced him by saying, "He is a poor man, but a good fellow, and is so like Louis XI to look at that we call him Louis the XIth." I remember that Verlaine talked of Victor Hugo who was "a supreme poet, but a volcano of mud as well as of flame," and of Villiers de L'Isle Adam who was "exalté" and wrote excellent French; and of In Memoriam, which he had tried to translate and could not. "Tennyson is too noble, too Anglais; when he should have been brokenhearted, he had many reminiscences."

At Verlaine's burial, but a few months after, his mistress quarrelled with a publisher at the graveside as to who owned the sheet by which the body had been covered, and Louis XI stole fourteen umbrellas that he found leaning against a tree in the Cemetery.

XIX

I am certain of one date, for I have gone to much trouble to get it right. I met John Synge for the first time in the Autumn of 1896, when I was one and thirty, and he four and twenty. I was at the Hotel Corneille instead of my usual lodging, and why I cannot remember for I thought it expensive. Synge's biographer says that you boarded there for a pound a week, but I was accustomed to cook my own breakfast, and dine at an anarchist restaurant in the Boulevard S. Jacques for little over a shilling. Someone, whose name I forget, told me there was a poor Irishman at the top of the house, and presently introduced us. Synge had come lately from Italy, and had played his fiddle to peasants in the Black Forest; six months of travel upon fifty pounds; and was now reading French literature and writing morbid and melancholy verse. He told me that he had learned Irish at Trinity College, so I urged him to go to the Aran Islands and find a life that had never been expressed in literature, instead of a life where all had been expressed. I did not divine his genius, but I felt he needed something to take him out of his morbidity and melancholy. Perhaps I would have given the same advice to any young Irish writer who knew Irish, for I had been that summer upon Inishmaan and Inishmore, and was full of the subject. My friends and I had landed from a fishing boat to find ourselves among a group of islanders, one of whom said he would bring us to the oldest man upon Inishmaan. This old man, speaking very slowly, but with laughing eyes, had said, "If any gentleman has done a crime, we'll hide him. There was a gentleman that killed his father, and I had him in my own house six months till he got away to America."

From that on I saw much of Synge, and brought him to Maude Gonne's, under whose persuasion perhaps, he joined the "Young Ireland Society of Paris," the name we gave to half a dozen Parisian Irish, signed, but resigned after a few months because "it wanted to stir up Continental nations against England, and England will never give us freedom until she feels she is safe," the one political sentence I ever heard him speak. Over a year was to pass before he took my advice and settled for a while in an Aran cottage, and became happy, having escaped at last, as he wrote, "from the squalor of the poor and the nullity of the rich." I almost forget the prose and verse he showed me in Paris, though I read it all through again when after his death I decided, at his written request, what was to be published and what not. Indeed, I have but a vague impression, as of a man trying to look out of a window and blurring all that he sees by breathing upon the window. According to my Lunar parable, he was a man of the twenty-third Phase, a man whose subjective lives, for a constant return to our life is a part of my dream, were over, who must not pursue an image, but fly from it, all that subjective dreaming, that had once been power and joy, now corrupting within him. He had to take the first plunge into the world beyond himself, the first plunge away from himself that is always pure technique, the delight in doing, not because one would or should, but merely because one can do.

He once said to me, "a man has to bring up his family and be as virtuous as is compatible with so doing, and if he does more than that he is a puritan; a dramatist has to express his subject and to find as much beauty as is compatible with that, and if he does more he is an aesthete," that is to say, he was consciously objective. Whenever he tried to write drama without dialect he wrote badly, and he made several attempts, because only through dialect could he escape self-expression, see all that he did from without, allow his intellect to judge the images of his mind as if they had been created by some other mind. His objectivity was, however, technical only, for in those images paraded all the desires of his heart. He was timid, too shy for general conversation, an invalid and full of moral scruple, and he was to create now some ranting braggadocio, now some tipsy hag full of poetical speech, and now some young man or girl full of the most abounding health. He never spoke an unkind word, had admirable manners, and yet his art was to fill the streets with rioters, and to bring upon his dearest friends enemies that may last their lifetime.

No mind can engender till divided into two, but that of a Keats or a Shelley falls into an intellectual part that follows, and a hidden emotional flying image, whereas in a mind like that of Synge the emotional part is dreaded and stagnant, while the intellectual part is a clear mirror-like technical achievement.

But in writing of Synge I have run far ahead, for in 1896 he was but one picture among many. I am often astonished when I think that we can meet unmoved some person, or pass some house, that in later years is to bear a chief part in our life. Should there not be some flutter of the nerve or stopping of the heart like that Macgregor experienced at the first meeting with a phantom?

XX

Many pictures come before me without date or order. I am walking somewhere near the Luxembourg Gardens when Synge, who seldom generalises and only after much thought, says, "There are three things any two of which have often come together but never all three; ecstasy, asceticism, austerity; I wish to bring all three together."

I notice that Macgregor considers William Sharp vague and sentimental, while Sharp is repelled by Macgregor's hardness and arrogance. William Sharp met Macgregor in the Louvre, and said, "No doubt considering your studies you live upon milk and fruit." And Macgregor replied, "No, not exactly milk and fruit, but very nearly so;" and now Sharp has lunched with Macgregor and been given nothing but brandy and radishes.

Macgregor is much troubled by ladies who seek spiritual advice, and one has called to ask his help against phantoms who have the appearance of decayed corpses, and try to get into bed with her at night. He has driven her away with one furious sentence, "Very bad taste on both sides."

I am sitting in a Café with two French Americans, one in the morning, while we are talking wildly, and some are dancing, there is a tap at the shuttered window; we open it and three ladies enter, the wife of a man of letters, who thought to find no one but a confederate, and her husband's two young sisters whom she has brought secretly to some disreputable dance. She is very confused at seeing us, but as she looks from one to another understands that we have taken some drug and laughs; caught in our dream we know vaguely that she is scandalous according to our code and to all codes, but smile at her benevolently and laugh.

I am at Stuart Merrill's, and I meet there a young Jewish Persian scholar. He has a large gold ring, seemingly very rough, made by some amateur, and he shows me that it has shaped itself to his finger, and says, "That is because it contains no alloy, it is alchemical gold." I ask who made the gold, and he says a certain Rabbi, and begins to talk of the Rabbi's miracles. We do not question him, perhaps it is true, perhaps he has imagined at all, we are inclined to accept every historical belief once more.

I am sitting in a Cafe with two French Americans, a German poet Douchenday, and a silent man whom I discover to be Strindberg, and who is looking for the Philosopher's Stone. The French American reads out a manifesto he is about to issue to the Latin Quarter; it proposes to establish a communistic colony of artists in Virginia, and there is a footnote to explain why he selects Virginia, "Art has never flourished twice in the same place. Art has never flourished in Virginia."

Douchenday, who has some reputation as a poet, explains that his poems are without verbs, as the verb is the root of all evil in the world. He wishes for an art where all things are immoveable, as though the clouds should be made of marble. I turn over the page of one of his books which he shows me, and find there a poem in dramatic form, but when I ask if he hopes to have it played he says: "It could only be played by actors before a black marble wall, with masks in their hands. They must not wear the masks for that would not express my scorn for reality."

I go to the first performance of Alfred Jarry's Ubu Roi, at the Théatre de L'Oeuvre, with the Rhymer who had been so attractive to the girl in the bicycling costume. The audience shake their fists at one another, and the Rhymer whispers to me, "There are often duels after these performances," and he explains to me what is happening on the stage. The players are supposed to be dolls, toys, marionettes, and now they are all hopping like wooden frogs, and I can see for myself that the chief personage, who is some kind of King, carries for Sceptre a brush of the kind that we use to clean a closet. Feeling bound to support the most spirited party, we have shouted for the play, but that night at the Hotel Corneille I am very sad, for comedy, objectivity, has displayed its growing power once more. I say, "After Stephane Mallarmé, after Paul Verlaine, after Gustave Moreau, after Puvis de Chavannes, after our own verse, after all our subtle colour and nervous rhythm, after the faint mixed tints of Conder, what more is possible? After us the Savage God."

BOOK V

THE STIRRING OF THE BONES

I

It may have been the Spring of 1897 that Maud Gonne, who was passing through London, told me that for some reason unknown to her, she had failed to get a Dublin authorization for an American lecturing tour. The young Dublin Nationalists planned a monument to Wolfe Tone which, it was hoped, might exceed in bulk and in height that of the too compromised and compromising Daniel O'Connell, and she proposed to raise money for it by these lectures. I had left the Temple and taken two rooms in Bloomsbury, and in Bloomsbury lived important London Nationalists, elderly doctors, who had been medical students during the Fenian movement. So I was able to gather a sufficient committee to pass the necessary resolution. She had no sooner sailed than I found out why the Dublin committee had refused it, or rather put it off by delay and vague promises. A prominent Irish

American had been murdered for political reasons, and another Irish American had been tried and acquitted, but was still accused by his political opponents, and the dispute had spread to London and to Ireland, and had there intermixed itself with current politics and gathered new bitterness. My committee, and the majority of the Nationalist Irish Societies throughout England were upon one side, and the Dublin committee and the majority of the Nationalist Societies in Ireland upon the other, and feeling ran high. Maud Gonne had the same friends that I had, and the Dublin committee could not be made to understand that whatever money she collected would go to the movement, and not to her friends and their opponents. It seemed to me that if I accepted the Presidency of the '98 Commemoration Association of Great Britain, I might be able to prevent a public quarrel, and so make a great central council possible; and a public quarrel I did prevent, though with little gain perhaps to anybody, for at least one active man assured me that I had taken the heart out of his work, and no gain at all perhaps to the movement, for our central council had commonly to send two organizers or to print two pamphlets, that both parties might be represented when one pamphlet or one organizer had served.

II

It was no business of mine, and that was precisely why I could not keep out of it. Every enterprise that offered, allured just in so far as it was not my business. I still think that in a species of man, wherein I count myself, nothing so much matters as Unity of Being, but if I seek it as Goethe sought, who was not of that species, I but combine in myself, and perhaps as it now seems, looking backward, in others also, incompatibles. Goethe, in whom objectivity and subjectivity were intermixed I hold, as the dark is mixed with the light at the eighteenth Lunar Phase, could but seek it as Wilhelm Meister seeks it intellectually, critically, and through a multitude of deliberately chosen experiences; events and forms of skill gathered as if for a collector's cabinet; whereas true Unity of Being, where all the nature murmurs in response if but a single note be touched, is found emotionally, instinctively, by the rejection of all experience not of the right quality, and by the limitation of its quantity. Of all this I knew nothing, for I saw the world by the light of what my father had said, speaking about some Frenchman who frequented the dissecting rooms to overcome his dread in the interest of that Unity. My father had mocked, but had not explained why he had mocked, and I, for my unhappiness had felt a shuddering fascination. Nor did I understand as yet how little that Unity, however wisely sought, is possible without a Unity of Culture in class or people that is no longer possible at all.

"The fascination of what's difficult
Has dried the sap out of my veins, and rent
Spontaneous joy and natural content
Out of my heart."

III

I went hither and thither speaking at meetings in England and Scotland and occasionally at tumultuous Dublin conventions, and endured some of the worst months of my life. I had felt years before that I had made a great achievement when the man who trained my uncle's horses invited me to share his Xmas dinner, which we roasted in front of his harness room fire; and now I took an almost equal pride in an evening spent with some small organizer into whose spitoon I secretly poured my third glass of whiskey. I constantly hoped for some gain in self-possession, in rapidity of decision, in capacity for disguise, and am at this moment, I dare say, no different for it all, having but burgeoned and withered like a tree.

When Maud Gonne returned she became our directing mind both in England and in Ireland, and it was mainly at her bidding that our movement become a protest against the dissensions, the lack of dignity, of the Parnellite and Anti-Parnellite parties, who had fought one another for seven or eight years, till busy men passed them by, as they did those performing cats that in my childhood I used to see, pretending to spit at one another on a table, outside Charing Cross station. Both parliamentary parties seeing that all young Ireland, and a good part of old, were in the movement, tried to join us, the Anti-Parnellite without abandoning its separate identity. They were admitted I think, but upon what terms I do not remember. I and two or three others had to meet Michael Davitt, and a member of parliament called F. X. O'Brien to talk out the question of separate identity, and I remember nothing of what passed but the manner and image of Michael Davitt. He seemed hardly more unfitted for such negotiation, perhaps even for any possible present politics, than I myself, and I watched him with sympathy. One knows by the way a man sits in his chair if he have emotional intensity, and Davitt's suggested to me a writer, a painter, an artist of some kind, rather than a man of action. Then, too, F. X. O'Brien did not care whether he used a good or a bad argument, whether he seemed a fool or a clever man, so that he carried his point, but if he used a bad argument Davitt would bring our thought back to it though he had to wait several minutes and re-state it. One felt that he had lived always with small unimaginative, effective men whom he despised; and that perhaps through some lack of early education, perhaps because nine years' imprisonment at the most plastic period of his life had jarred or broken his contact with reality, he had failed, except during the first months of the Land League, to dominate those men. He told me that if the split in the Irish Party had not come he would have carried the Land League into the Highlands, and recovered for Ireland as much of Scotland as was still Gaelic in blood or in language. Our negotiations, which interested so much F. X. O'Brien and my two negotiators, a barrister and a doctor, bored him I thought, even more than they did me, to whom they were a novelty; but the Highland plan with its historical foundation and its vague possibilities excited him, and it seemed to me that what we said or did stirred him, at other moments also, to some similar remote thought and emotion. I think he returned my sympathy, for a little before his death he replied to some words of congratulation I sent him after the speech in which he resigned his seat in the House of Commons, with an account of some project of his for improving the quality of the Irish representation there.

IV

I think that he shared with poet and philosopher the necessity of speaking the whole mind or remaining silent or ineffective, and he had been for years in a movement, where, to adapt certain words of a friend of mine, it was as essential to carry the heart upon the sleeve as the tongue in the cheek. The founders of the Irish Agrarian movement had acted upon the doctrine, contradicted by religious history, that ignorant men will not work for an idea, or feel a political passion for its own sake, and that you must find "a lever" as it was called, some practical grievance; and I do not think that I am fantastic in believing that this faith in "levers," universal among revolutionaries, is but a result of that mechanical philosophy of the Eighteenth Century, which has, as Coleridge said, turned the human mind into the quicksilver at the back of a mirror, though it still permits a work of art to seem "a mirror dawdling along a road."

O'Leary had told me the story, not I think hitherto published. A prominent Irish American, not long released from the prison where Fenianism had sent him, cabled to Parnell: "Take up Land Reform side by side with the National Question and we will support you. See Kickham." What had Parnell, a landowner and a haughty man, to do with the peasant or the peasant's grievance? And he was indeed so ignorant of both that he asked Kickham, novelist and Fenian leader, if he thought the people would take up a land agitation, and Kickham answered: "I am only afraid they would go to the Gates of Hell for it;" and O'Leary's comment was, "and so they have."

And so was founded an agitation where some men pretended to national passion for the land's sake; some men to agrarian passion for the nation's sake; some men to both for their own advancement, and this agitation at the time I write of had but old men to serve it, who found themselves after years of labour, some after years of imprisonment, derided for unscrupulous rascals. Unscrupulous they certainly were, for they had grown up amid make-believe, and now because their practical grievance was too near settlement to blind and to excite, their make-believe was visible to all. They were as eloquent as ever, they had never indeed shared anything in common but the sentimental imagery, the poetical allusions inherited from a still earlier generation, but were faced by a generation that had turned against all oratory. I recall to my memory a member of Parliament who had fought for Parnell's policy after Parnell's death, and much against his own interest, who refused to attend a meeting my friends had summoned at the declaration of the Boer War, because he thought "England was in the right," and yet a week later when the Dublin mob had taken the matter up, advised Irish soldiers to shoot their officers and join President Kruger. I recall another and more distinguished politician who supported the Anti-Parnellite Party in his declining years, and in his vigorous years had raked up some scandal about some Colonial Governor. A friend of mine, after advising that Governor's son to write his father's life, had remembered the scandal and called in her alarm upon the politician; "I do beseech you," he had said and with the greatest earnestness, "to pay no attention whatever to anything I may have said during an election."

Certain of these men, all public prepossessions laid aside, were excellent talkers, genial and friendly men, with memories enriched by country humour, and much half sentimental, half practical philosophy, and at moments by poetical feeling that was not all an affectation, found very moving by English sympathisers, of the tear and the smile in Erin's eye. They may even have had more sincerity than their sort elsewhere, but they had inherited a cause that men had died for, and they themselves had gone to jail for it, and had so worn their hereditary martyrdom that they had seemed for a time no common men, and now must pay the penalty. "I have just told Mahaffy," Wilde had said to me, "that it is a party of men of genius," and now John O'Leary, Taylor, and many obscure sincere men had pulled them down; and yet, should what followed, judged by an eye that thinks most of the individual soul, be counted as more clearly out of the common? A movement first of poetry, then of sentimentality, and land hunger, had struggled with, and as the nation passed into the second period of all revolutions, had given way before a movement of abstraction and hatred; and after some twenty years of the second period, though abstraction and hatred have won their victory, there is no clear sign, of a third, a tertium quid, and a reasonable frame of mind.

Seeing that only the individual soul can attain to its spiritual opposite, a nation in tumult must needs pass to and fro between mechanical opposites, but one hopes always that those opposites may acquire sex and engender. At moments when I have thought of the results of political subjection upon Ireland I have remembered a story told me by Oscar Wilde who professed to have found it in a book of magic, "if you carve a Cerberus upon an emerald," he said, "and put it in the oil of a lamp and carry it into a room where your enemy is, two heads will come upon his shoulders and devour one another."

Instead of sharing our traditional sentimental rhetoric with every man who had found a practical grievance, whether one care a button for the grievance or not, most of us were prosecuting heretics. Nationality was like religion, few could be saved, and meditation had but one theme, the perfect nation and its perfect service. "Public opinion," said an anonymous postcard sent to a friend of mine, "will compel you to learn Irish," and it certainly did compel many persons of settled habits to change tailor and cloth. I believed myself dressed according to public opinion, until a letter of apology from my tailor informed me that "It takes such a long time getting Connemara cloth as it has to come all the way from Scotland."

The Ireland of men's affections must be, as it were, self-moving, self-creating, though as yet (avoiding a conclusion that seemed hopeless) but few added altogether separate from England politically. Men for the moment were less concerned with the final achievement than with independence from English parties and influence during the struggle for it. We had no longer any leaders, abstractions were in their place; and our Conventions, where O'Leary presided interrupting discussion without the least consideration for rules of procedure when the moment came for his cup of coffee, were dominated by little groups, the Gaelic propagandists, though still very few, being the most impassioned, which had the intensity and narrowness of theological sects.

I had in my head a project to reconcile old and new that gave Maud Gonne and myself many stirring conversations upon journeys by rail to meetings in Scotland, in Dublin, or in the Midlands. Should we not persuade the organizations in Dublin and in London, when the time drew near for the unveiling of our statue, or even perhaps for the laying of its foundation stone, to invite the leaders of Parnellite or Anti-Parnellite, of the new group of Unionists who had almost changed sides in their indignation at the over-taxation of Ireland, to lay their policy before our Convention, could we not then propose and carry that the Convention sit permanently, or appoint some Executive Committee to direct Irish policy and report from time to time. The total withdrawal from Westminster had been proposed in the 'Seventies, before the two devouring heads were of equal strength, and now that the abstract head seemed the strongest, would be proposed again, but the Convention could send them thither, not as an independent power, but as its delegation, and only when, and for what purpose the Convention might decide. I dreaded some wild Fenian movement, and with literature perhaps more in my mind than politics, dreamed of that Unity of Culture which might begin with some few men controlling some form of administration. I began to talk my project over with various organizers, who often interrupted their attention which was perhaps only politeness, with some new jibe at Mr. Dillon or Mr. Redmond. I thought I had Maud Gonne's support, but when I overheard her conversation, she commonly urged the entire withdrawal of the Irish Members, or if she did refer to my scheme, it was to suggest the sending to England of eighty ragged and drunken Dublin beggars or eighty pugilists "to be paid by results."

She was the first who spoke publicly or semi-publicly of the withdrawal of the Irish Members as a practical policy for our time, so far as I know, but others may have been considering it. A nation in crisis becomes almost like a single mind, or rather like those minds I have described that become channels for parallel streams of thought, each stream taking the colour of the mind it flows through. These streams are not set moving, as I think, through conversation or publication, but through "telepathic contact" at some depth below that of normal consciousness, and it is only years afterwards, when future events have shown the themes' importance, that we discover that they are different expressions of a common theme. That self-moving, self-creating nation necessitated an Irish centre of policy, and I planned a premature impossible peace between those two devouring heads because I was sedentary and thoughtful; but Maud Gonne was not sedentary, and I noticed that before some great event she did not think but became exceedingly superstitous. Are not such as she aware, at moments of great crisis, of some power beyond their own minds; or are they like some good portrait painter of my father's generation and only think when the model is under their eye? Once upon the eve of some demonstration, I found her with many caged larks and finches which she was about to set free for the luck's sake.

I abandoned my plans on discovering that our young men, not yet educated by Mr. Birrell's university, would certainly shout down everyone they disagreed with, and that their finance was so extravagant that we must content ourselves with a foundation stone and an iron rail to protect it, for there could never be a statue; while she carried out every plan she made.

Her power over crowds was at its height, and some portion of the power came because she could still, even when pushing an abstract principle to what seemed to me an absurdity, keep her own mind free, and so when men and women did her bidding they did it not only because she was beautiful, but because that beauty suggested joy and freedom. Besides there was an element in her beauty that moved minds full of old Gaelic stories and poems, for she looked as though she lived in an ancient civilization where all superiorities whether of the mind or the body were a part of public ceremonial, were in some way the crowd's creation, as the Pope entering the Vatican is the crowd's creation. Her beauty, backed by her great stature, could instantly affect an assembly, and not as often with our stage beauties because obvious and florid, for it was incredibly distinguished, and if, as must be that it might seem that assembly's very self, fused, unified, and solitary, her face, like the face of some Greek statue, showed little thought, her whole body seemed a master work of long labouring thought, as though a Scopas had measured and calculated, consorted with Egyptian sages, and mathematicians out of Babylon, that he might outface even Artemisia's sepulchral image with a living norm.

But in that ancient civilization abstract thought scarce existed, while she but rose partially and for a moment out of raging abstraction; and for that reason, as I have known another woman do, she hated her own beauty, not its effect upon others, but its image in the mirror. Beauty is from the antithetical self, and a woman can scarce but hate it, for not only does it demand a painful daily service, but it calls for the denial or the dissolution of the self.

"How many centuries spent
The sedentary soul,
In toil of measurement
Beyond eagle or mole
Beyond hearing and seeing
Or Archimedes' guess,
To raise into being
That loveliness?"

V

On the morning of the great procession, the greatest in living memory, the Parnellite and Anti-Parnellite members of Parliament, huddled together like cows in a storm, gather behind our carriage, and I hear John Redmond say to certain of his late enemies, "I went up nearer the head of the Procession, but one of the Marshals said, 'This is not your place, Mr Redmond; your place is further back.' 'No,' I said, 'I will stay here.' 'In that case,' he said, 'I will lead you back.'" Later on I can see by the pushing and shouldering of a delegate from South Africa how important place and procedure is; and noticing that Maud Gonne is cheered everywhere, and that the Irish Members march through street after street without welcome, I wonder if their enemies have not intended their humiliation.

We are at the Mansion House Banquet, and John Dillon is making the first speech he has made before a popular Dublin audience since the death of Parnell; and I have several times to keep my London delegates from interrupting. Dillon is very nervous, and as I watch him the abstract passion begins to rise within me, and I am almost overpowered by an instinct of cruelty; I long to cry out, "Had Zimri peace who slew his master?"

Is our Foundation Stone still unlaid when the more important streets are decorated for Queen Victoria's Jubilee?

I find Maud Gonne at her hotel talking to a young working-man who looks very melancholy. She had offered to speak at one of the regular meetings of his socialist society about Queen Victoria, and he has summoned what will be a great meeting in the open air. She has refused to speak, and he says that her refusal means his ruin, as nobody will ever believe that he had any promise at all. When he has left without complaint or anger, she gives me very cogent reasons against the open air meeting, but I can think of nothing but the young man and his look of melancholy. He has left his address, and presently at my persuasion, she drives to his tenement, where she finds him and his wife and children crowded into a very small space, perhaps there was only one room, and, moved by the sight, promises to speak. The young man is James Connolly who, with Padraic Pearce, is to make the Insurrection of 1916 and to be executed.

The meeting is held in College Green and is very crowded, and Maud Gonne speaks, I think, standing upon a chair. In front of her is an old woman with a miniature of Lord Edward Fitzgerald, which she waves in her excitement, crying out, "I was in it before she was born." Maud Gonne tells how that morning she had gone to lay a wreath upon a martyr's tomb at St. Michael's Church, for it is the one day in the year when such wreaths are laid, but has been refused admission because it is the Jubilee. Then she pauses, and after that her voice rises to a cry, "Must the graves of our dead go undecorated because Victoria has her Jubilee?"

It is eight or nine at night, and she and I have come from the City Hall, where the Convention has been sitting, that we may walk to the National Club in Rutland Square, and we find a great crowd in the street, who surround us and accompany us. Presently I hear a sound of breaking glass, the crowd has begun to stone the windows of decorated houses, and when I try to speak that I may restore order, I discover that I have lost my voice through much speaking at the Convention. I can only whisper and gesticulate, and as I am thus freed from responsibility, I share the emotion of the crowd, and perhaps even feel as they feel when the glass crashes. Maud Gonne has a look of exultation as she walks with her laughing head thrown back.

Later that night Connolly carries in procession a coffin with the words "British Empire" upon it, and police and mob fight for its ownership, and at last that the police may not capture, it is thrown into the Liffey. And there are fights between police and window-breakers, and I read in the morning papers that many have been wounded; some two hundred heads have been dressed at the hospitals; an old woman killed by baton blows, or perhaps trampled under the feet of the crowd; and that two thousand pounds worth of decorated plate glass windows have been broken. I count the links in the chain of responsibility, run them across my fingers, and wonder if any link there is from my workshop.

Queen Victoria visits the city, and Dublin Unionists have gathered together from all Ireland some twelve thousand children and built for them a grandstand, and bought them sweets and buns that they may cheer. A week later Maud Gonne marches forty thousand children through the streets of

Dublin, and in a field beyond Drumcondra, and in the presence of a Priest of their Church, they swear to cherish towards England until the freedom of Ireland has been won, an undying enmity.

How many of these children will carry bomb or rifle when a little under or a little over thirty?

Feeling is still running high between the Dublin and London organizations, for a London doctor, my fellow-delegate, has called a little after breakfast to say he was condemned to death by a certain secret society the night before. He is very angry, though it does not seem that his life is in danger, for the insult is beyond endurance.

We arrive at Chancery Lane for our Committee meeting, but it is Derby Day, and certain men who have arranged a boxing match are in possession of our rooms. We adjourn to a neighbouring public-house where there are little pannelled cubicles as in an old-fashioned eating house, that we may direct the secretary how to answer that week's letters. We are much interrupted by a committee man who has been to the Derby, and now, half lying on the table, keeps repeating, "I know what you all think. Let us hand on the torch, you think, let us hand it on to our children, but I say no! I say, let us order an immediate rising."

Presently one of the boxers arrives, sent up to apologise it seems, and to explain that we had not been recognized. He begins his apology but stops, and for a moment fixes upon us a meditative critical eye. "No, I will not," he cries. "What do I care for anyone now but Venus and Adonis and the other Planets of Heaven."

French sympathisers have been brought to see the old buildings in Galway, and with the towns of Southern France in their mind's eye, are not in the least moved. The greater number are in a small crowded hotel. Presently an acquaintance of mine, peeping, while it is still broad day, from his bedroom window, sees the proprietress of the hotel near the hall door, and in the road a serious-minded, quixotic Dublin barrister, with a little boy who carries from a stick over his shoulder twelve chamber pots. He hears one angry, and one soft pleading explanatory voice, "But, Madam, I feel certain that at the unexpected arrival of so many guests, so many guests of the Nation, I may say, you must have found yourself unprepared." "Never have I been so insulted." "Madam, I am thinking of the honour of my country."

I am at Maud Gonne's hotel, and an Italian sympathiser Cipriani, the friend of Garibaldi, is there, and though an old man now, he is the handsomest man I have ever seen. I am telling a ghost story in English at one end of the room, and he is talking politics in French at the other. Somebody says, "Yeats believes in ghosts," and Cipriani interrupts for a moment his impassioned declamation to say in English, and with a magnificent movement and intonation, "As for me, I believe in nothing but cannon."

I call at the office of the Dublin organization in Westmoreland Street, and find the front door open, and the office door open, and though the office is empty the cupboard door open and eighteen pounds in gold upon the shelf.

At a London Committee meeting I notice a middle-aged man who slips into the room for a moment, whispers something to the secretary, lays three or four shillings on a table, and slips out. I am told that he is an Irish board-school teacher who, in early life, took an oath neither to drink nor smoke, but to contribute the amount so saved weekly to the Irish Cause.

VI

A few months before I was drawn into politics, I made a friendship that was to make possible that old project of an Irish Theatre. Arthur Symons and I were staying at Tillyra Castle in County Galway with Mr. Edward Martyn, when Lady Gregory, whom I had met once in London for a few minutes drove over, and after Symon's return to London I stayed at her house, which is some four miles from Tillyra. I was in poor health, the strain of youth had been greater than it commonly is, even with imaginative men, who must always, I think, find youth bitter, and I had lost myself besides as I had done periodically for years, upon Hodos Camelionis. The first time was in my eighteenth or nineteenth years, when I tried to create a more multitudinous dramatic form, and now I had got there through a novel that I could neither write nor cease to write which had Hodos Camelionis for its theme. My chief person was to see all the modern visionary sects pass before his bewildered eyes, as Flaubert's St. Anthony saw the Christian sects, and I was as helpless to create artistic, as my chief person to create philosophic order. It was not that I do not love order, or that I lack capacity for it, but that, and not in the arts and in thought only, I outrun my strength. It is not so much that I choose too many elements, as that the possible unities themselves seem without number, like those angels, that in Henry More's paraphrase of the Schoolman's problem, dance spurred and booted upon the point of a needle. Perhaps fifty years ago I had been in less trouble, but what can one do when the age itself has come to Hodos Camelionis?

Lady Gregory seeing that I was ill brought me from cottage to cottage to gather folk-belief, tales of the fairies, and the like, and wrote down herself what we had gathered, considering that this work, in which one let others talk, and walked about the fields so much, would lie, to use a country phrase, "Very light upon the mind." She asked me to return there the next year, and for years to come I was to spend my summers at her house. When I was in good health again, I found myself indolent, partly perhaps because I was affrighted by that impossible novel, and asked her to send me to my work every day at eleven, and at some other hour to my letters, rating me with idleness if need be, and I doubt if I should have done much with my life but for her firmness and her care. After a time, though not very quickly, I recovered tolerable industry, though it has only been of late years that I have found it possible to face an hour's verse without a preliminary struggle and much putting off.

Certain woods at Sligo, the woods above Dooney Rock and those above the waterfall at Ben Bulben, though I shall never perhaps walk there again, are so deep in my affections that I dream about them at night; and yet the woods at Coole, though they do not come into my dream are so much more knitted to my thought, that when I am dead they will have, I am persuaded, my longest visit. When we are dead, according to my belief, we live our lives backward for a certain number of years, treading the paths that we have trodden, growing young again, even childish again, till some attain an innocence that is no longer a mere accident of nature, but the human intellect's crowning achievement. It was at Coole that the first few simple thoughts that now, grown complex, through their contact with other thoughts, explain the world, came to me from beyond my own mind. I practised meditations, and these, as I think, so affected my sleep that I began to have dreams that differed from ordinary dreams in seeming to take place amid brilliant light, and by their invariable coherence, and certain half-dreams, if I can call them so, between sleep and waking. I have noticed that such experiences come to me most often amid distraction, at some time that seems of all times the least fitting, as though it were necessary for the exterior mind to be engaged elsewhere, and it was during 1897 and 1898, when I was always just arriving from or just setting out to some political meeting, that the first dreams came. I was crossing a little stream near Inchy Wood and actually in the middle of a stride from bank to bank, when an emotion never experienced before swept down upon me. I said, "That is what the devout Christian feels, that is how he surrenders his will to the will of God." I felt an extreme surprise for my whole imagination was preoccupied with the pagan mythology of ancient Ireland, I was marking in red ink upon a large map, every sacred mountain. The next morning I awoke near dawn, to hear a voice saying, "The love of God is infinite for every human soul because every human soul is unique, no other can satisfy the same need in God."

Lady Gregory and I had heard many tales of changelings, grown men and women as well as children, who as the people believe are taken by the fairies, some spirit or inanimate object bewitched into their likeness remaining in their stead, and I constantly asked myself what reality there could be in these tales, often supported by so much testimony. I woke one night to find myself lying upon my back with all my limbs rigid, and to hear a ceremonial measured voice which did not seem to be mine speaking through my lips, "We make an image of him who sleeps," it said, "and it is not him who sleeps, and we call it Emmanuel." After many years that thought, others often found as strangely being added to it, became the thought of the Mask, which I have used in these memoirs to explain men's characters. A few months ago at Oxford I was asking myself why it should be "An image of him who sleeps," and took down from the shelf not knowing why I was doing so, a book which I had never read, Burkitt's Early Eastern Christianity, and opened it at random. My eyes lit upon a passage from a Gnostic Hymn telling how a certain King's son being exiled, slept in Egypt, a symbol of the natural state, and while he slept an Angel brought him a royal mantle; and at the bottom of the page I found a footnote saying that the word mantle did not represent the meaning properly for that which the Angel gave had the exile's own form and likeness. I did not, however, find in the Gnostic Hymn my other thought that Egypt and that which the Mask represents are antithetical. That, I think, became clear, though I had had some premonitions when a countryman told Lady Gregory and myself that he had heard the crying of new-dropped lambs in November, Spring in the world of Fairy, being November with us.

On the sea coast at Duras, a few miles from Coole, an old French Count, Florimond de Bastero, lived for certain months in every year. Lady Gregory and I talked over my project of an Irish Theatre looking out upon the lawn of his house, watching a large flock of ducks that was always gathered for his arrival from Paris, and that would be a very small flock, if indeed it were a flock at all, when he set out for Rome in the autumn. I told her that I had given up my project because it was impossible to get the few pounds necessary for a start in little halls, and she promised to collect or give the money necessary. That was her first great service to the Irish intellectual movement. She reminded me the other day that when she first asked me what she could do to help our movement I suggested nothing; and, certainly, no more foresaw her genius that I foresaw that of John Synge, nor had she herself foreseen it. Our theatre had been established before she wrote or had any ambition to write, and yet her little comedies have merriment and beauty, an unusual combination, and those two volumes where the Irish heroic tales are arranged and translated in an English so simple and so noble, may do more than other books to deepen Irish imagination. They contain our ancient literature, are something better than our Mabinogion, are almost our Morte D'Arthur. It is more fitting, however, that in a book of memoirs I should speak of her personal influence, and especially as no witness is likely to arise better qualified to speak. If that influence were lacking, Ireland would be greatly impoverished, so much has been planned out in the library, or among the woods at Coole; for it was there that John Shawe Taylor found the independence from class and family that made him summon the conference between landlord and tenant, that brought land purchase, and it was there that Hugh Lane formed those Irish ambitions that led to his scattering many thousands, and gathering much ingratitude; and where, but for that conversation at Florimond de Bastero's, had been the genius of Synge?

I have written these words instead of leaving all to posterity, and though my friend's ear seems indifferent to praise or blame, that young men to whom recent events are often more obscure than those long past, may learn what debts they owe and to what creditor.

William Butler Yeats – A Short Biography

William Butler Yeats (1865 – 1939) is best described as Ireland's national poet in addition to being one of the major twentieth-century literary figures of the English tongue. To many literary critics, Yeats represents the 'Romantic poet of modernism,' which is quite revealing about his extraordinary style that combines between the outward emphasis on the expression of emotions and the extensive use of symbolism, imagery and allusions. Yeats also wrote prose and drama and established himself as the spokesman of the Irish cause. His fame was greatly boosted mainly after he received the Nobel Prize in Literature in 1923. His life was marked by his many love stories, by his great interest in oriental mysticism and occultism as well as by political engagement since he served as an Irish senator for two terms. Today, although William Butler Yeats's contribution to literary modernism and to Irish nationalism remains incontestable, his poetic oeuvre represents his finest achievement and will always be part and parcel of the English poetic canon.

William Butler Yeats was born in the year 1865 in the Irish capital Dublin to be raised by a family that historically had a passion for the arts. Young Yeats received his earlier education at home before the family moved to London where he never forgot his passion for Irish Gaelic culture, language, and mythology. The latter were to haunt him throughout his whole life and to find their way to his most acknowledged verse. One may venture to say that Yeats inherited the poetic and Romantic talents of such poets as Edmund Spencer, John Donne, Percy Bysshe Shelley, and William Blake while adding to his verse a flavor of Irish lore. Yeats was only two years when the family settled in London. This was mainly in order to enable his elder siblings to pursue their artistic careers. In addition to the formal education that he received at the Godolphin School, Yeats was continuously instructed by his mother and by his brother John who focused mainly on experimental sciences.
The family's stay in London was interrupted, though. They had to return to Dublin in the early 1880s where the teenage Irish man attended Erasmus Smith High School and then the National College of Art and Design. They remained there until 1887 when they went back to London anew. It was during those years that Yeats, while making acquaintances with a number of writers and painters, started to arrange his earliest poetic lines. A number of prose writings and poems were published in the *Dublin University Review*. Later, some Irish publication houses started to publish Yeats's works which combined between verse and prose. For instance, in 1886 Yeats combined between poetry and drama in the play *Mosada* while two years later he published a volume entitled Fairy and Folk Tales of the Irish Peasantry. His first poetic volume was published in 1889 under the title *The Wanderings of Oisin and Other Poems*. Many readers and critics agree that Yeats's early writings were

particularly influenced by Shelley, Spencer and then William Blake. The presence of Irish mythology and folklore is to fade away in the later phase of his career.

In 1890, while publishing one of his most successful and acknowledged poems entitled "The Lake Isle of Innisfree," Yeats launched a poetry club with a group of fellow poets that used to meet at a local tavern to exchange ideas and recitals of their modernist poetry. The group was given the name "The Rhymers' Club" and had achieved a considerable reputation in London. By the 1890s, Yeats started to produce profuse and diversified writings. These included, but were not limited to, *Irish Faerie Tales* (1892), *The Countess Kathleen and Various Legends and Lyrics* (1892), a play entitled *The land of Heart's Desire* (1894) and more than one volume of short stories and poetry. Yeats continuously combined between poetry, fiction and drama. He wrote drama in verse as well as narrative poetry drawing on mythology and popular folktales.

Yeats remained very prolific during the rest of his life. In the 1900s, more poetry volumes and plays followed as well as non-fictional writings in the style of philosophical reflections and spiritual contemplations such as *Ideas of Good and Evil* (1903) and Discoveries (1907). While the second phase of Yeats's career as a poet was conventionally marked by his gradual detachment from the classic and the Romantic schools, it showed his great interest in oriental mysticism, spiritualism and occultism. The poet was seriously concerned with this esoteric world that he wanted to explore and fully understand. While being influenced by the works of the Swedish theologian and mystic Emanuel Swedenborg, Yeats took part in different clubs and associations that were interested in the paranormal. He and his fellow organized séances and claimed that they interacted with ghosts and spirits. By and large, critics and biographers maintain divergent views on the impact of such interest on the value and merits of the poet's oeuvre. Some harshly criticize Yeats and dismiss his interest in the occult as "nonsense" and some believe that it represents a serious and respectable exploration of the dark and unmapped world of the metaphysical.

Earlier in 1899, Yeats's passion for theatre made him found with a number of fellow playwrights and intellectuals the Abbey Theatre, or The National Theatre of Ireland in the city of Dublin. This enabled him to perform his own experimental plays as well as plays by others that sought to establish an Irish theatrical tradition.

In the 1910s, Yeats's style became more sophisticated and his style reached an unprecedented degree of beauty and refinement. This manifests itself in poems such as "Easter, 1916" published in the eponymous year and "The Wild Swans at Coole" first published in 1917, then revised in 1919. In 1920, Yeats published what many still consider as his most brilliant poetic achievement under the title "The Second Coming." The style of Yeats's later poems was marked by the heavy use of symbolism and imagery in addition to its respect of rhyme and meter. Yeats mainly developed a tendency towards the extensive use of illusions. References to glorious and dignified events, places and characters such as the Trojan wars, Byzantium, Greek and Christian mythologies are frequent in his verse and led to a revival of this old tradition in the modern epoch. Most critics distinguish between Yeats and his contemporaries and personal friends Ezra Pound and T. S. Eliot, regarding the first as representing a traditionalist tendency among the modernist.

Moreover, it is seldom enough to insist on Yeats's spiritual and mystic side which was greatly reflected in his later writings. Yeats's exploration of the spiritual world and the nature of the divine and the soul was a life-time quest and while leaving its traces in most of his remarkable works, it culminated in the publication of *A Vision* in 1925. Other successful works that appeared in Yeats's later years included his play *The Resurrection* (1927) and the volume of poetry entitled *The Tower* (1928) which included the very famous "Sailing to Byzantium." Interestingly, Yeats continued writing until his last days and the most important achievement of his final years was probably *The Winding Stair and Other Poems* published in 1933.

Being a rather romantic gentleman and obviously a handsome man, women had a special impact on Yeats's life as well as on his literary works. His name and reputation were mainly associated with one woman that he had supposedly loved throughout his whole life, Maud Gonne. The latter was a beautiful lady much concerned with the cause of Irish nationalism. Yeats was so infatuated with Gonne that he repeatedly proposed to her, but in vain. Apparently, the poet was not ardent enough to please the young lady who felt much more committed to her cause than to him. She married the Irish nationalist Major John MacBride instead. The friendship of the couple persisted, though, and she maintained her status as an inspirational muse for the poet all along his career.

Nevertheless, Yeats was an Irish nationalist too. He was probably just less convinced of pure militancy and was more inclined towards artistic resistance. It is equally noteworthy that Yeats belonged to the Protestant minority in Ireland and had a very critical stance on the Catholicism of the majority. He seemingly hated the general association of Irish nationalism with the Catholic Church as a symbol of national identity and distinction from the English, an association that Gonne was drawn to. These details did never alienate the poet from his sense of nationalism which was later reconfirmed when he was hailed by the Nobel Prize committee as the poet of the Irish nation. Yeats's nationalism was also recognized by his native country when he was appointed to the first Irish Senate in 1922 and then in 1925. In addition to Maud Gonne, Yeats also knew other women from the intellectual and artistic circles that he frequented, most of whom are way younger than him. These included Olivia Shakespear and Georgie Hyde Lees who became his wife in 1917.

In 1928, Yeats started to have serious health problems and was forced to leave the Senate. Yet, he soon recovered, mainly after undergoing an operation in 1934. He spent the remaining years of his existence publishing prolifically and having more romantic affairs with younger women. He also edited and published anthologies of modern poetry that were to mark those extraordinary decades of the twentieth century. It was on January 28th, 1939 that William Butler Yeats died in Menton, France. Following his personal wish, he was first buried in the French town of Roquebrune-Cap-Martin to be later moved and re-interred at Drumcliff, County Sligo in Ireland where he spent some of his childhood years.

www.ingramcontent.com/pod-product-compliance
Lightning Source LLC
Chambersburg PA
CBHW072017170626
46813CB00005B/2167